FORGIVING
THE ANGEL

FORGIVING THE ANGEL

FOUR STORIES FOR FRANZ KAFKA

JAY CANTOR

 ALFRED A. KNOPF · NEW YORK · 2014

THIS IS A BORZOI BOOK
PUBLISHED BY ALFRED A. KNOPF

All rights reserved. Published in the United States by Alfred A. Knopf,
a division of Random House LLC, New York, and in Canada by Random House
of Canada Limited, Toronto, Penguin Random House Companies.
www.aaknopf.com

Knopf, Borzoi Books, and the colophon are
registered trademarks of Random House LLC.

Library of Congress Cataloging-in-Publication Data
Cantor, Jay.
  [Short stories. Selections]
  Forgiving the angel : four stories for Franz Kafka / Jay Cantor.
          pages   cm
  Summary: "From one of our most admired and thought-provoking writers: a
brilliant, beautifully written, sometimes heart-wrenching gathering of fictionalized
stories that center on a circle of real people whose lives were in some way shaped by
their encounters with Franz Kafka"— Provided by publisher.
  ISBN 978-0-385-35034-1 (Hardcover)
  1. Kafka, Franz, 1883–1924—Fiction. I. Title.
  PS3553.A5475A6   2013
  813'.54—dc23   2013016747

Jacket illustration by Guy Billout
Jacket design by Chip Kidd

Manufactured in the United States of America
First Edition

For Stanley Cavell—to acknowledge,
with gratitude, the sustaining friendship
of someone whose life and work have seen
so deeply into the nature of friendship,
acknowledgment, and gratitude.

CONTENTS

FORGIVING
THE ANGEL

1

MORE THAN ONCE, Franz Kafka told his close friend and literary executor, Max Brod, that when Kafka died, Brod was to burn all his unpublished manuscripts. Brod, though, disobeyed his friend's instructions, and not long after Kafka's death, he arranged for the publication of Kafka's abandoned novels, and then, over time, his stories, parables, and even his diaries and letters.

The things of Kafka's that Brod had never published are now in safe-deposit boxes in Jerusalem and Zurich, and will remain there until a court decides who owns them. At dispute is whether Brod left the papers to his secretary, Esther Hoffe, as an *executor* who was to carry out Brod's wish that they be conveyed to the Israeli National Library—*if* that was his wish—or if he left them as her property, which she could sell, if she wanted, to whoever might pay the most, even to a library of the German nation.

In the Jerusalem courtroom, lawyers speaking on behalf

of Esther Hoffe's daughters (who have inherited the papers from their mother, if, that is, they have, indeed, inherited them) have argued that no one should open the boxes before their ownership is determined, or even for a time afterward. They propose to sell the manuscripts unseen— if there are manuscripts in the boxes. "If we get an agreement, the material will be offered for sale as a single entity, in one package. It will be sold by weight. . . . There's a kilogram of papers here." The material might be new stories, diaries, or minor things altogether (for Brod prized every scrap by Kafka, even the notes from when Kafka was so sick he could not speak, was perhaps no longer making sense, and wrote things like a *top hat made of water.*)

"The highest bidder," the lawyers said, "will then be able to open the boxes and see what's there. The National Library can get in line and make an offer, too."

Absurd perhaps, though as we'll see, that's not altogether the fault of the lawyers. But to tell you how the papers came to be in sealed boxes that are to be sold by weight, I must tell you a story.

2

THAT STORY BEGINS in Berlin in 1923, less than a year before Kafka's death, with a visit from Max Brod. Kafka, who had once complained that life was a train trip toward death that had far too many intervening stops for his taste, now would embrace a doctor if he said Kafka was looking a little better.

They'd had news like that recently. Kafka told Brod confidently that when the tuberculosis receded a little more, and he became "transportable," he and Dora Diamant, the woman he lived with in Berlin, would move to Palestine. In Tel Aviv, they'd open a restaurant where Kafka would be the waiter, Dora the cook. Kafka had put a white towel over his arm, and smiled with a combination of servility and the servant's mean-spirited cunning. He looked, Brod thought, a little ridiculous, but that was never something that seemed to bother Franz.

"I suggest you order our soup," Dora said.

"Particularly tasty?" Brod said.

"No, fortunately for you, we have no soup today. You see, our waiter is very likely to spill any bowls we trust him with."

"Which is why they never give me any, even empty ones," Kafka said. "The ghosts might fill them on the way to your table, and I would certainly pour the contents on your clothes when I cough."

Kafka and Dora laughed and looked toward Max expectantly. Like lovers everywhere, they took so much pleasure in each other that they couldn't imagine one wouldn't join them.

Like lovers everywhere? Milena had once written Brod that "Franz has a fear of everything that's shamelessly alive," yet Franz wasn't afraid of Dora. Kafka had broken his engagement with Felice because when one writes even night isn't night enough, one requires the loneliness of the grave. Yet he'd written new stories in this small apartment while Dora sewed on the couch nearby.

An impresario might sell tickets to the spectacle: *Franz Kafka in Love*, the writer free of his father and the claws of Prague, and living with a woman who was seemingly at ease in her body.

But like the restaurant, it might only be a show. After all, how could Dora feel easy in Berlin? She'd run here from her Hasidic family, and her father had sat shiva over her. And why had she come here? *So she could study her father's Judaism.* How could a woman be so buoyant, if she revered what restricted and even despised her?

But she was. She'd even made Kafka avid to know more of his Judaism, and of her Hasidism, who believed (Franz had written him) that even the driest, most seemingly irrational mitzvah, if performed with the right intention, could open the gates of heaven. "Of course, all we poor people have now are the stories about those who had the right intention. Sometimes, though, the rabbis believe that if the story is told with the right intention, it suffices."

"So the tales of the wonder-working rabbis," Brod had replied, "are like . . . like something by Franz Kafka." Brod should have added: or they would be, if the Hasid imagined that men's intentions (or was it God's own?) were always hopelessly divided, and that even a story always came too early or too late.

Dora had brought the East to Kafka, and Franz the West to her, all its culture and literature. Yet at the same time, she'd decided (not wrongly, Brod thought, but on slender evidence on her part) that Franz was himself a new Master of the Good Name. The first Baal Shem, though, had a manual of what acts would knit body and soul together—the Talmud—while her lover's might fly apart at any moment if he didn't continue to look for the right stories to reknit things.

That afternoon, Brod had left them to go visit his pretty Berlin mistress. As he walked down the stairs, he heard them laughing again, companionably, not the least bit maliciously. He felt a chill at the sound. Max was a short man with an enormous head and a hunched back; he wore thick glasses on a prominent nose; he was far less handsome than Kafka (despite Franz's somewhat prominent ears). Until today, though, they had both thought Max was much the more successful with women (if *success* meant *endless entanglement*). Max felt he'd given Kafka hope by being a misshapen man who still could trust and take pleasure in life. With Dora, Kafka, for the time—and may it be a long one—had both. Franz no longer needed Max.

3

OR PERHAPS he only didn't need him to enact romance for him; fortunately for Max, he still had other uses. Brod had already published thirty-seven books of his own, knew editors at all the German-language publishers, journals, and newspapers. Kafka, who Brod usually had to beg and cajole to publish anything, now grasped eagerly at Brod's help in placing his work. Franz had only a small pension from his job at the Accident Insurance Bureau, and needed to earn money to support himself and Dora.

When Brod came to Berlin for his second visit, Kafka had been, in a familiar gesture, leaning against the wall, each (Kafka had once said) holding the other one up. His tailored suit hung on him as if he were—

"I know," he said, reading Max's mind. "I look like a walking stick for a giant."

Kafka, over 1.8 meters tall, weighed 53 kilos. And even if Franz were paid in crowns for his story, it would only be enough for a few days food, or one visit from a mediocre doctor—if, that is, they managed to spend the notes quickly enough after they converted the crowns to marks. Prices would double even as they took ten steps away from the bank. Franz, Brod thought, might be killed by tuberculosis, but it would be a murder, too, one perpetrated by the War, and the vengeance it had brought on Germany.

"But Max, you worry about me too much. I've put on fifty grams already this week. My sister sent me a package of Prague butter, and Dora made me the most remarkable meal with it—and on nothing but that spirit lamp."

Dora was bent over that "stove" now, making coffee for them. Kafka looked fondly toward her, and she, as if she could feel his eyes on her, gazed back toward him for a moment with a singleness of concentration that made Brod understand what it meant to be the apple of someone's eye. This made him say, "Oh, why couldn't the Hunger Artist also find something he liked to eat"—that being the story whose galleys he held in his hands. Brod was thinking not of the Prague butter, of course, but the greater miracle, the round-faced woman from Poland.

"Ah, but the Hunger Artist's career would already have made him more of an outcast than those American performers who bite the heads off poultry," Franz said, immediately, as if he'd already considered this possibility. "Once he started eating, no one would give him another job, and no one would be willing to teach him a new skill. He'd soon be a Hunger Artist again, *malgré lui*."

"Which makes his situation," Dora said, her back to them both again, "like any man who has nothing to sell but his labor. Prices go up, wages go down, and the food he can afford soon brings less new strength than he used getting the money to pay for his food." Dora had fled to Berlin to read Talmud for herself but had encountered socialism along the way. She didn't sound doctrinaire, though, but musing, like someone testing the reality of a formula for herself.

At her words Kafka's eyes widened, and his face took on another kind of sadness. He'd seen the spark inside Dora, one that, like the tuberculosis bacillus, might also burst into a flame and consume her life. It was as if, Brod thought (years later and under his own sky), Franz had seen her life in the KDP, her flight to the Soviet Union and then away from it, seen that not in its terrifying particulars, of course, but like a broad shadow passing over the earth.

"You know," Franz said to Brod, "you must eventually burn the story you're holding in your hand."

"That's beyond my powers," Brod said. "What I hold are proof sheets of the story for you to correct. This story's about to be published."

"You're right, of course. Now, let's hope that to mock my wish, the Malevolent doesn't set to work destroying Europe's libraries."

"Or its readers," Dora added, having learned from a master.

"The demons don't need an excuse to destroy," Brod

said. "Best, though, that your work is here to sustain us when they do appear." At that, he wondered (and not for the first time) why he'd never envied Franz his genius. Perhaps because to write like Franz Kafka, one would have to be Franz Kafka, and that hadn't been bearable for anyone, even Franz Kafka. Until now, that is.

"Still," Kafka said, "you must do your part and burn my remaining papers."

Brod looked to Dora for help. "He isn't appointing me his literary executor," he said, "but his literary executioner." Max knew he was perhaps too pleased with the cleverness of this, but his cry was heartfelt as well.

Dora, however, nodded her agreement with Franz. She didn't know what priceless things they were talking about, as she hadn't read a whit of Kafka's writing from before he met her. All botched, he'd said, and though she didn't believe that, she didn't seek his work out, either; she had his presence, and didn't need to possess his past. "He believes that burning the papers will keep the ghosts from coming after him anymore."

Brod knew this was insane, and yet such was his belief in Franz's intuitions about the manifold and hidden connections of things that he also worried that Franz might be right. After he left that day, Brod planned to consult a psychoanalyst about himself, and then see the demanding mistress who was the reason he needed the doctor. He wondered what a therapist who had studied with Kafka would be like. Perhaps you would tell him a dream and, as in a fairy tale, he would hand you a lizard. Or clip your nails.

"Make Dora your executor," he said, annoyed with

them both, but not meaning it, as, after all, she might burn Franz's work.

"No. She loves me differently than you, Max. You're the person to do this for me."

In the meantime, Dora had finished her conjuring over the spirit lamp. She offered Franz a cup, and held out a glass to Brod.

The coffee tasted bitter, but it had been made by a woman who was unambivalently in love. What powers might such a potion have?

4

NONE FOR BROD. His mistress threatened to take up with a straight-backed gentile man if he didn't leave his wife. And though the Gospels might say that love was stronger than death, it still remained weaker than German inflation. Kafka and Dora had chased prices up and down Berlin's streets and avenues, but they hadn't caught up with them before Franz had run out of breath. Franz had to return to his bedroom in the family flat in Prague. Here, Brod and he plotted out where he might send the work he'd written in Berlin, and so raise enough money that he could escape from his father's house—a horror to which he wouldn't expose Dora—and rejoin his beloved in Germany.

"This story," Franz said (it was "A Little Woman"), "will have to hide itself in the world. The others will have an easier time of it, though. Those, you'll burn."

"No," Max said. "I won't." He steeled himself. The world, he knew, would thank him for his great refusal.

"Max, you're an honest man, and I am proud to call you my dearest friend. I know you can't ignore my dying request."

Franz Kafka's dearest friend. Brod felt deeply honored. How could he not do as Franz asked? "I most certainly can and will ignore your request," Max said. "I won't do it." Franz Kafka's works would be like a well of water for the world, and yes, Max, would benefit, too. This role, saving Franz's stories, might be the difference between his endless, grinding *career,* and doing something truly worthwhile, something that would be remembered.

As if in reply, Kafka described a small revision he would like made to one of the unpublished, and therefore supposedly to be destroyed, manuscripts. Max felt as though Kafka was teasing him. If so, the activity must give Kafka a little ease, and so, as his closest friend, Brod would simply have to bear it.

And strangely, just after Brod had had this thought, Kafka said, "Do you think the ebb and flow of pain means the Angel of Death is playing with me, the way a cat plays with a captured mouse?"

"Cruel, that cat," Brod said, also meaning Kafka Kat toward Max Mouse.

"Cruel, yes," Kafka said, "but not malign. The teasing is probably more meant to ease the torment the cat feels than to add to the pain of the mouse."

This made Brod sure that Kafka's disease had, if such

a thing were possible, increased his sensitivity, allowed him to read Brod's mind even more clearly than he had before, when Kafka had often understood him without Brod's knowing how, and in a way that saw his concerns in their purity—the ambiguous gift of such vision being that Max's worries, seen that way, became crushing insoluble burdens, and he could no longer imagine anymore what wine he might rightfully drink if there was no one to pray to Who might bless it.

"But why," Brod asked, "does the cat need to distract himself from his joy in his meal?"

"Joy? Oh, no. Cats loath having to earn their wages by killing mice, who in themselves are not only living beings like the cat, but in addition have for them the thoroughly bitter taste of the cat's servitude."

"How awful for the both of them, then."

"Worse for the mouse."

"Yes, it's about to die." Max had lost track for a moment which of the two of them was the rodent.

"Not only that. The mouse must forgive the cat his death as well. After all, by hunting and eating mice, the cat is doing what it must to get a place indoors. Cats seem so sublimely indifferent to everyone only so they might bear with dignity their sense of the depth of this degrading slavery."

"And the Angel of Death?"

"He's just like the cat. He does his Master's bidding, but he hates his work. Who else would God have chosen for the task? If He employed an Angel who rejoiced in vengeance, humanity wouldn't have lasted an instant. Instead, God chose an Angel of the greatest sensitivity, one who feels every death to the core of his being. So we shouldn't begrudge the Angel the momentary distraction he gets from tormenting us. Of course, he also takes a little revenge on us, too. After all, isn't it the man himself who forced the Angel to do this hateful thing by being unfit for life?"

Forgiving the Angel had exhausted Kafka this afternoon. He closed his eyes. Brod stood by him for a moment before he left, to make sure he was asleep. But as he got to the door, he heard Kafka's barely audible voice. The most considerate of men, who knew how busy Brod was (between mistresses, wife, and work), nearly demanded that he come to visit the next day.

By then, in an almost superhuman effort, Franz had finished "Josephine, the Singer," who by the strength of her demand convinces her mouse folk that her wheezing is sublime song. "I think," Kafka whispered, "that I may have started the investigation of animal squeaking at the right moment." Some ghost had whittled away his voice, and when he tried to moisten it with fruit juice, his throat burst into flame. They pretended not to know what that meant. Brod, Kafka said, must place this story as soon as possible to pay something of the cost of a sanatorium at the Wienerwald, where Franz could receive treatment—and be with Dora again for however long he had left.

5

AT THE SANATORIUM, he and Max went over the galleys for that story and prepared the other things that he'd written in Berlin to pay for treatment and, Franz said, for their life in Berlin after. Franz weighed less than 45 kilos and ran a fever without cease. He was in agony swallowing not just with fruit juice but from water. Yet he and Dora, each for the sake of the other, pretended that recovery, and a return to their life in Berlin, might still be possible.

Dora sat by the bed, delicately offering Franz a spoon-ful of water. Franz lay flatter as the spoon went in, and his face contorted, as if a shard of glass was stuck in his throat and dug more deeply into the tender skin when he tried to swallow this boulder. Dora looked down at him with a pride and love strangely untouched by pity, as if Kafka were a brave soldier and not even one wounded and in hospital, but one still in battle.

That afternoon the doctor came and, not bound as the three of them were, told Franz the truth, that he had tubercular lesions of the larynx. He would need more serious treatment than this sanatorium could provide—at the least, alcohol injections into the nerve and perhaps surgery—or he would die of dehydration and starvation. He recommended the university clinic of Professor Hajek in Vienna, where, he said, sometimes miracles had been performed.

Had they, Brod wondered, or was it unbearable, even to this man who hardly knew him, that Kafka might die?

6

AT HAJEK'S CLINIC Dora could be with him during the day, but at night she wasn't there to protect him. Franz had a bed in a ward like a cell, where he lay between other tubercular patients. "This morning," she wrote to Brod, "he pointed to the bed of a jovial man who'd died the night before. Franz was not shaken but positively angry, as if he could not grasp that the man who had been so gay had to die. I cannot forget his malicious, ironic smile." At Kafka's own expense, Brod supposed, if he believed in God, and at God's expense, if He believed in His own goodness.

It was a rare night in the ward, when there wasn't occasion for that smile. Dora felt sure the place would kill Franz—kill him faster, one should say—if they couldn't get him a room of his own. Franz, though, didn't believe he'd the right to ask for a special privilege, thought himself only a nearly nameless sailor who in better times had simply held to his desk all night. His only skill, he'd once told Brod, was to cling to the wood with sufficient desperation.

Brod may have found this a little disingenuous, but Dora respected his view of himself. She didn't try to use Kafka's reputation (such as it was at that point), only demanded—with a piercing purity of spirit that even a demon couldn't refuse—that Dr. Hajek give Franz a room of his own because "he was a person of the greatest sensitivity."

Dr. Hajek looked down at his chart—no doubt to remind himself of the patient's name—and said that whatever his sensitivities, Franz Kafka would be treated no differently than any other patient.

Franz, to spare his voice, sometimes scribbled things on slips of paper, and perhaps it was in response to Hajek's refusal that he wrote to Max when he arrived:

It occurs to me that I am not like other people, though I pretend to be. Of course, that I can pretend probably shows that I am very much like other people, for that is no doubt what they are doing, too.

That day Max also saw the spectacle of a nurse spraying Kafka's larynx with menthol, and a doctor stabbing him there with an injection of alcohol. Kafka shivered like a tree hit by an ax, but for a little while after he could swallow again, and he ate a few strawberries and cherries. He smelled them for a long time first.

The relief lasted a few hours. By the evening Kafka wrote Brod a note: *To think that I was once able to manage a big sip of water.* He gave a malicious smile at his or God's expense, and asked if he might watch Max swallow some wine on his behalf, so he might experience drinking.

Brod complied, tried to indicate with his eyes how wonderfully tasty the wine was for him. Or was that cruel? Again, Max had had the good fortune to have Kafka contrive a problem for him that could have no right answer.

"I must ask your forgiveness, Max," Kafka whispered, again having read Brod's mind. "I deceived you before."

"Unlikely." He had never known Franz to lie.

"Well, let's say, then, that sometimes I have a hard time getting to the point."

"I thought that was part of your point."

"You are so kind, so generous, Max. It's impossible not to love you." Franz looked delighted to be naming Max's good qualities.

And then, very seriously and apologetically, he said, "I should have told you, Max, that the real reason the cat teases the mouse is to prepare him."

"Prepare him? For what? For the afterlife, you mean?"

"Oh, I doubt there is any. And if there is, I doubt there's any preparation for it. No, for this one. After all, the mouse the cat teases is the one most likely to escape."

Did his friend hope that Death, having teased him so much, would now withdraw? "Then what has the mouse learned from his education?" Brod said. "Beware of cats?"

Franz opened his eyes and raised his shoulders in bewilderment, more likely at what was about to overcome him than at Brod's question. He grasped the glass flask from the table in his long, expressive fingers and began to convulse with coughs. Dora ran to put her arms behind him. He filled the flask with bloody sputum.

Brod felt sure he'd understood what Kafka had meant. The cat tormented the rodent, and let him escape because he wanted to be remembered by someone, even a mouse, and even as a tormentor. He wept a bit to think that Franz Kafka imagined Max Brod could ever forget him.

When the coughing finished, a doctor and a nurse came with the syringe for Kafka's larynx. This time they made Brod leave the room.

7

FOR FRANZ, the deaths in the beds near him were far less bearable than the silver needle plunged into his decaying throat. Franz and Dora contradicted Dr. Hajek's orders and moved him to Dr. Hoffman's sanatorium. They each said that they believed that the private room there, filled with bundles of flowers Dora would gather, the balcony with sunshine and fresh air, and the vegetarian meals, might effect a cure. Did either of them really think that? Or did each say that for the sake of the other, so they could make Kafka's last weeks comfortable?

Brod, too, had lied. He said he had to be in Austria for the premiere of an opera, and not so he might say farewell to Franz. The man who most loved truth, Brod thought, found himself, when dying, surrounded by lies, albeit loving ones.

A few weeks previously, Franz had written to Dora's father, saying that he was not a practicing Jew, but one who was honestly repentant. He asked him for permission to marry his daughter. The morning of the afternoon Brod had arrived, they'd received a letter; Dora's father had carried Franz's note on the long journey to the Gerrer Rebbe. The rabbi read it, put it to one side, and said, "No."

"This *no*," Brod said, "changes nothing." After all, Franz and Dora had already joined themselves together more than any man or wife he knew, himself and Elsa most certainly included.

And yet the rabbi's refusal had changed everything for Franz, who was certain that the wonder rabbi had pronounced this judgment because he knew Kafka would die soon.

Dora argued that the rabbi had said *no* to punish her for having run away from paternal authority.

"Or," Brod added, "it's because Franz is not a Hasid."

Kafka stared at them with characteristic astonishment, then slowly wrote:

Such is the power of a no *that comes without justification. It gathers into itself all the reasons one might suspect for why one should rightly be refused. And who could be a better prosecutor in this matter than one's self?*

"If," Brod said, "one is Franz Kafka."

Kafka had smiled in that ironic and malicious way that now terrified Max, since it seemed to call both God and Kafka's right to live into question. In response to the rabbi's judgment that he would die soon, Brod knew Franz would set himself to work at dying soon.

As if in response to that thought, Kafka passed Brod a note, with a revision of the title of one of the stories he'd written in Berlin. Why scribble, and with such painful difficulty, of a change to a manuscript that was supposed to be burnt? But Brod didn't ask that, afraid that it might lead to Franz repeating that he was to burn his work, words that would send a flood of bile into Brod's throat.

Brod had left the room, and Dora came up behind him in the corridor, handed him another note Kafka had written her that morning: *How long will you be able to stand it? How long will I be able to stand your standing it?* Dora wept, and Brod—even as he embraced her—put the note in his jacket pocket.

8

MANY YEARS LATER, Brod and his terrified wife ran to the station to catch what would probably be the last train to leave Prague before the murderers arrived. Like Brod, almost everyone in the oddly silent crowd—as quiet as an audience just before the orchestra begins—clutched a suitcase or two of their treasures. For Brod, that meant some of Kafka's papers that he hadn't been able to send ahead, fragments of stories, little notes from when Franz could no longer talk, like, *Here it is nice to give people a drop of wine, because everyone is a little bit of a connoisseur, after all.* And even the letter, too, that Max had found when he'd cleaned out the drawers in Kafka's desk in Prague: *Dearest Max, My last request: Everything I leave behind me in the way of diaries, manuscripts, letters (my own and others), sketches and so on, to be burned unread,* which he saved because all of Kafka's papers were precious to him, even the one that confirmed that he'd betrayed Kafka's last wish by not burning his precious papers.

Max hardly ever thought of that vow he'd never made, but today he had the ridiculous feeling that the things in his suitcase were stolen, and that the people on the platform had decided that this crime was responsible for their predicament. They might gather round him and Elsa and forbid them to get on the train.

But who anymore, he reminded himself—or who but for the Nazis—wanted Franz Kafka's great work to have been destroyed? Only Dora Diamant, perhaps. She didn't care about Franz's reputation, had no desire that anyone else should read him. She opposed every publication—even after Max had the royalties made over to her. "Nobody," she said, "can get even an inkling of what he was about unless they knew him personally." She was a selfish widow, he wanted to tell his accusers on the platform. But Kafka was a great dark forest, and no one, not even Dora, could know all of it or keep it for themselves.

By the time the train arrived, Max's bad mood had passed, and he'd gathered up his strength again. The people on the platform began to push forward with an implacable wavelike motion, but Max swung the dangerous suitcases and cleared some space. He got on the train, pulled his wife up immediately after, and found a seat for her.

The train soon got under way, and, overcome by terror and relief, Max felt both lightheaded and nauseated. He gazed down at his precious Elsa, the reluctant Zionist. She lacked the spark, he thought sadly, that made the difficult Dora Diamant always want a commitment to something greater than herself. But the murderers had made the decision for Elsa and Max; and now they would make a life building the one place where they surely would both belong, the Jewish homeland.

9

THOUGH PERHAPS they didn't belong there together. Many years later, Max sat sullenly in his study in Tel Aviv after too much wine and another fight with his wife, one that was the more embarrassing because it had happened right outside a restaurant, after a party given in his honor as the director of the Habima Theatre. Anyone in the company might have heard them.

The fight had been his doing. He'd been afraid all evening she'd discover his affair with an actress at the theater who looked (for reasons that fascinated his analyst) a little like Dora Diamant, and so he'd naturally started an argument with Elsa, saying she no longer had any passion for him, meaning (but unsaid) that someone did, thus betraying the thing he meant to hide.

"My God, Max," Elsa had said, "what do you want from me after twenty years?"

He barely became hard with her anymore, but blamed her for that, though it was true with Hannah, too. (After all, Dora's looks weren't really to his taste.) "Even at the beginning," he'd said to her, "you only ever cared about my fame."

She laughed at him. "Your reputation?" she said. "For directing a provincial theater in this provincial desert, where, like Ben-Gurion said, even the actresses are Jewish whores?"

He felt more wounded by the insult to him than worried by this clear sign that she already knew of his affair. Still, he'd managed skillfully to make her the one who cried. By the time they'd gotten home she'd been raking her own cheeks with her long fingernails, drawing blood, and had run upstairs screaming (as she often did) that she never wanted to see him again.

As she left him, though, the room got larger and larger, and he got smaller and smaller, and he felt bereft and helpless. He shifted about completely. He wanted to be reassured that no matter what might happen with Elsa—*would she actually leave him?*—he *had* made a name for himself, that people could see him, and might be attracted to him.

He looked to his desk and saw the bright red-and-green cover of his new novel. In response, the book spun about a little—the effect of wine, or its anxiety for itself. Would anyone be attracted to it? He told the book, "I've published forty-eight volumes, you know," as if that should reassure it, rather than the reverse, given that most of those books were out of print and forgotten. The book only spun faster, turning brown.

Like rot. This novel would never give Brod a place in people's minds. Nor would the theater. Nor would his music. No, to the world only one of his titles mattered: Franz Kafka's literary executor, the man who'd refused to fulfill his friend's last wish. The world's gratitude usually drowned out any slight uneasiness about that. Probably the platform and the suitcases had been the last time the thing not done had made him truly uneasy. But tonight he'd made his wife dig at her own face with her fingernails—*again*—and the two betrayals mixed together in his stomach, like red and green, making a nauseating shit-colored mixture.

He could never defend himself to Franz against Franz's accusation that he hadn't acted like a friend, hadn't filled his clearly stated last wish. He couldn't offer Franz better reasons to save his work than Kafka had given him for destroying it, *because Franz had never said* why he wanted his work destroyed. He'd only pronounced his absolute judgment, and, like the Gerrer Rebbe, offered no justification for it.

He had a better chance to defend himself to his wife. He ran steadily up the stairs to the bedroom, clinging all the while to the tipsy banister. He resolved (again) that he'd break it off with Hannah at rehearsals on Monday. He would plead piteously and sincerely to Elsa. He'd promise that he would never again give her cause to doubt him, if she would only let him return to their bed, where he could feel the warmth of her body, and her acceptance of his.

10

A YEAR LATER, the night Elsa died in that same bed, Max had cried and moaned like a beaten animal. He couldn't have survived her death if it hadn't been for the support of his dear secretary, Esther Hoffe, a woman with a pleasant bosom, a fuller figure, but an equally matter-of-fact manner to his wife. She had tended his many manuscripts through to publication, arranged his appointments, and though she was married, had also tended him, had responded to Max as a man (which was, he had to admit, all the sweeter, really, because she was married).

But after her husband died, he and Esther hadn't married. He had felt loved by her, but not wanted (or was it the other way round?). Esther, like Elsa, lacked that purity of concentration that Dora had had, that he thought could make him feel he had been *seen*. So his own eye wandered, looking for another eye to look back at him.

With dissatisfaction and a wandering eye came the usual scarifying arguments, wounds, calluses, coldness. On the afternoon the very well-known Italian interviewer had called asking for him, he'd been glad for the distraction.

"I'm Max Brod," he'd said, but as he did, he'd felt that that wasn't really his name. Perhaps this unsettling effect on her subjects was part of what made her so successful as a journalist. He'd been intrigued by his unease, and, in return, he wanted to intrigue her, win over this famously beautiful woman. An admiring interview done by her would add his name to her distinguished list of subjects, so that it might become Fidel Castro, Sartre, De Gaulle, Mao, Max Brod.

Two days later, they met in his study, where he'd carefully placed all seventy of his books on the shelf just behind the chair where he sat—one of two large armchairs he had set in front of his desk, to show that he wasn't the sort to insist on position.

The woman who walked into this room, and almost immediately asked for an ashtray, was even better looking than her pictures. She had lustrous black hair that framed piercing eyes, and lovely long legs that she boldly showed off with a short skirt. She was young, yes—but was she really utterly too young for him, or his prostate?

She set a suitcase-sized tape recorder to work beside her. He was glad for it. Max looked forward to defending his view of Kafka's themes to her, doing battle against Adorno and Benjamin, who'd said Brod made Kafka too religious a figure; once and for all he'd put on record the amazing spiritual qualities of his friend.

"Dora Diamant," the interviewer began, surprisingly enough, "loved Franz Kafka."

"Yes, and he loved her." This made him remember the two of them performing, and Dora saying, *"No, fortunately for you, we have no soup today."* Franz had stood stiffly beside her, a white waiter's towel over his arm, and something innocent and foolish about his grin. If Kafka had recovered and he and Dora had lived together longer, would they have the sort of problems he'd had with Elsa? With Esther? He didn't rejoice in his friend's death, but he very much didn't want him to have had those problems, either.

"Perhaps Dora Diamant loved Franz Kafka more than anyone else did, even you."

"Yes." Of what might she be accusing him? Not loving Franz enough? That was not a charge that any court would take seriously.

"And she burnt his work."

Did the woman really imagine he hadn't considered that? The Italian's beauty was real enough, but her skill as an interrogator was dubious. "Kafka was alive then," he said, "and he ordered her to do it. What choice did she have? If she hadn't, he would have dragged his own body out of bed by the scruff of his own neck and done the burning himself."

"Dora said Kafka told her to destroy the manuscripts to keep the ghosts from attacking him. Don't you think that you may have left Kafka defenseless, open to the attack of tormenting demons?"

"Do you believe in ghosts, Miss?"

"No, but Kafka did."

"Yes, but he didn't believe in the afterlife. The demons, he knew, were all here on earth. That's why—before he met Dora Diamant—he'd longed for the peace of the grave."

"But isn't reputation an afterlife for a writer? Perhaps he didn't want to be judged by us. Perhaps we're the demons he feared."

Again, old news. "No one else's opinion mattered to Franz. His *no* thundered so loudly in his ears that he couldn't hear another judgment, even if it were shouted by a multitude."

"And he had said that *no*. And you ignored him."

"But Franz's *no* was for himself, and to himself. *If* there was an Absolute, then Franz felt he must testify that there was an unbridgeable distance between *him* and *it*. To keep God alive *for himself,* he had to say *no* to what *he* could accomplish—he couldn't finish so many of his things; and he had to say that *no* against himself all the way to the end, and even beyond it. Anything else would have called the Absolute into question for him, and that would have harmed the very mechanism that produced Kafka's work. When my friend died, *that* machine could no longer operate, and I could publish what he left."

"That sounds clever," she said, almost indifferently.

Max could feel his chest growing damp. He could take

off his jacket, but that would reveal what his tailor had worked so hard to hide. "In truth," he said—

"Yes, please, let's have the truth."

"In truth, I was never so very sure Franz meant me to burn his work. He would sometimes tell me to destroy something even as he told me to revise the title. Why would he have wanted me to make corrections to things that would be burnt?"

She dropped her cigarette in the ashtray, breathed in avidly. "You've convinced me."

For the first time, he saw pleasure in her eyes. Max knew immediately that he'd fallen into a trap.

"He didn't want his work burnt. The question then is, why would Franz Kafka give you, Max Brod, this job that he knew you wouldn't perform? Why would your friend put a knife in your conscience like that?"

More his stomach than his conscience, Max thought. He often felt like he'd something hard in his belly that he could neither digest or excrete. It rubbed and rubbed against the insides, producing endless amounts of bile.

Even now, he could taste it. Why *had* Franz done this to *him*? Why tell *him* to do something Max had said he wouldn't do? He remembered Franz's description of Kafka Kat tormenting Max Mouse. "I think Franz gave me this task that he knew I wouldn't perform so I'd always remember him. Only a law one wants to fulfill but can't because it conflicts with another law one also wants to fulfill keeps God before our eyes."

"We aren't talking about God, Mr. Brod, but a fallible man. And that man couldn't have thought you much of a friend, if he thought he had to do all that to be remembered by you."

At that, Max Mouse's eyes grew moist. He wiped them like a child with his sleeve, looking to see if her face softened.

It didn't. "I think," she said, "that you're making yourself ridiculous by avoiding the obvious explanation. Franz Kafka wanted the world to remember him as someone who believed in the Absolute, someone indifferent to audience or reputation, but he also, much more strongly, wanted to have the immortality and fame that would result from his work. So he told you to burn the work, while knowing that he'd prepared you not to do it."

Prepared. That was the word Kafka had used. But what she'd said couldn't possibly be true. He'd never seen Franz be duplicitous or selfish with a friend. Or with *anyone.*

But what might a man do at the last moment, to ensure his good name for eternity?

"No, no, no, no," Max said. He covered his face with his hands and wept in earnest.

"Oh, yes, I can certainly see that vanity and meanness would be particularly hard for you to accept in someone that you—as Benjamin and Adorno have written—have spent a lifetime making into a religious writer, even something of a saint."

Could it be so simple, so obvious? Had he missed it only because he'd been blinded by his love for Franz, and—like his own wives had been toward his lies—wouldn't let himself see how duplicitous one's beloved could be? That thought gave him cramps so terrible that he wanted to scream. With his head still buried in his hands, he barely noticed when the interviewer packed up her tape recorder and left.

11

HE PUT WHAT SHE'D SAID out of mind, not refuting it, not examining it. Six days after the interview, though, and still in some pain, Brod had been looking over some pages in Kafka's own hand, preparing a new volume of Franz's letters to friends and family. Pages lay scattered on his desk in piles, edges sticking out like wayward children. Overcome by an annoyance so great that it made the cramps worse, he picked up a handful of this paper, and without looking to see what was in it, he shoved it all into a brown accordion folder.

As soon as he did it, his stomach quieted, and he knew immediately that the pages must remain forever unread, though now that the world was as avid for anything Kafka as he'd always been (and yes, still was), he'd no idea how to keep them hidden, supposing he didn't actually burn them—which, even now, he would never do.

Still, from that moment on, for every thirty pages or so that he prepared for publication, he also put some paper into the folder without looking at it. Not the best things, perhaps—on the other hand, who knows, perhaps some were the best things. It was absolutely necessary that he *not* know that, and that no one ever knew.

Of course, sometimes he couldn't help it; his eye glanced down at what his hands did. Once, he saw some pages that could have been a lost story by Franz Kafka, which he felt particularly virtuous for not examining, and once a note from the sanatorium that he thought said *into the depths, in the deep harbors.* But he didn't stop and look further at any of it. These were *the destroyed pages,* the burnt things, and so not meant for anyone's eyes. Besides, if he didn't look, he could also hope that somewhere in the folder there was a strongly worded letter telling him *not* to burn his stories, perhaps even instructing him to publish them.

But publish Franz's diaries? His agonized letters to Felice? No, Franz would never have authorized those. Now that he'd even momentarily doubted Franz's good faith, though, nothing could stop him from publishing them, and so the world would benefit from Max's despair.

The folders worked nicely enough, too. He might occasionally be reminded of the unperformed command, or what the *demone italiano* had said about Kafka's motives; but if that soured his stomach, he need only blindly put one or two more pages in the folder, and he'd immediately feel some ease.

12

FOR A LONG WHILE, people who had a page of manuscript or letter by Kafka sent them to Max, so there'd always been new things for publication or for the folder. But in the last year, the stream of pages was finally drying up and at the same time the stomach pain and bile had grown much worse. He still treated them by shoveling a letter or two into the folder, but he had to ration the pages. Maybe it was too little; it didn't seem to help his stomach.

The last month, he had no appetite. He grew skinny, could trace the lump of thick bone that was his back as if it had only the thinnest covering of parchment. He'd no fecal matter when he defecated, but plenty of dark blood.

Esther noticed, of course. Max said his problems were caused by his being Kafka's literary executor. "The ghosts are finally coming after me." He smiled, though he had also meant it.

Esther had never heard the piercing conviction with which Kafka talked of these creatures, so she didn't take the ghosts seriously, which he felt was at once sensible and philistine of her. She made him see a doctor. Within the week, he'd been booked into the hospital for tests, and when they came back, into the operating theater for surgery.

13

THE DAY HE WAITED in his room for drugs to take hold so he could be wheeled under the knife, he heard squat, pugnacious Esther demand a private room for him when he returned.

"Beds are precious this week," the nurse said.

"Beds are always precious," Esther replied. "And so is your patient. He's Max Brod. He has published more than seventy volumes. He is the director of our national theater." Even through the haze of the drugs, Brod thought, *She hasn't made Dora's mistake.* Esther knew that sensitivity wasn't a currency that won protection for anyone.

The nurse looked down at his chart, as if to check the name. "The man who was Kafka's friend?"

Esther smiled. Perhaps, Max thought, Kafka made him his executor not to ensure Franz's own spurious sanctity, but so Max could get a private room after surgery.

14

AND AS THEY wheeled him into his single room after the operation, he was delighted to see what Kafka and Esther had obtained for him while he'd been under the knife. The room was spacious, with freshly painted white walls and a balcony where he might sun himself as he recovered. Esther must have gone somewhere to pick wildflowers. They filled every table and shelf.

15

WHEN HE AWOKE AGAIN, the drugs had worn off and he was in terrible pain. The walls of the room had turned sickly yellow, the balcony had evaporated, and the wildflowers had become arrangements ordered from florists, sent to him by well-wishers, theater companies, publishers—organizations more than individuals. They had a lacquered look, like Esther's hair as she sat by his bed, putting entries in a ledger.

When she saw he was awake and staring at her, she said he should try to take a little soup, even held a spoonful out for him. Max felt as though he'd swallowed a ball of fire, but to please her he slowly bent forward toward the spoon—until he saw the look of pity in her eyes for a very sick man. That disgusted him. It provided further evidence for the obvious: he wasn't in Vienna but Tel Aviv, dying of stomach cancer, not tuberculosis, and this woman's affection for him was in no way like Dora Diamant's love for Franz Kafka.

Here, however, morphine was freely available, and the drug allowed him a serenity, almost a shrug to these discoveries. Had the seeming perfection of Dora's and Franz's love, he wondered calmly, made him always deprecate what he had? Thus his affairs.

Don't be silly. After years of analysis, he knew it was the

hump. If a woman accepted him into her bed, he thought he might believe he wasn't deformed. But no, for some reason, the strategy failed; he couldn't believe it; and so . . . on to the next. That meager insight, he thought, had cost him years on the couch, thousands of shekels, and done nothing to change him or to make him feel as good as morphine did.

His surgeon came through the door, as if pushing against a strong wind. "You've clean-shaven cheeks," Max said, "but I can see from your expression that you are my Gerrer Rebbe."

Esther and the doctor looked bewildered.

"We opened him up," the doctor said—not to him, though, but to Esther—"and what we found inside . . . well, we just had to close him up again."

"Can I take him home?" Esther said. They spoke as if Max had lost the power of speech. Apparently, to be condemned to death was like being turned into a bug.

"If you think you can keep him comfortable."

16

SHE DID. She found light cotton blankets, pillows for his bed, and nurses for the day, who came with bedpans, sponges for baths, and all the other necessary equipment involved in modern dying.

People came to say goodbye, some as individuals, some

as representatives of organizations; one or two, also, who had been his lovers. He was annoyed by how little the representatives knew him, and Esther was annoyed by the former lovers, and as she was his sole support now, that made the visits not worth the bother. He asked Esther to put them off.

A day or two after that, Esther, practical as always, said, "What should I do with the things in the folders?" Esther was like him—one who arranged for publication, who got the best price, who managed to immigrate to Palestine. She was sensible. Still, her attitude gave him a pang. She valued him, but mainly because he was a source of support for her.

"You mean the burnt things—"

"What? No, I mean the brown folders in your study, the ones with Kafka's papers in them."

He felt anxious that she knew about them, but he had the presence of mind to tell her that no one must see those things while either of them were alive. "The world would despise you for revealing them," he said; and, as he didn't know what was inside the folders, maybe what he'd said was true. Maybe Kafka had done unspeakable things—besides making Max his executor. He doubted it, though. He probably had saved all his meanness for his supposed best friend, his dupe, his front man for sainthood.

"Sell the manuscript to *The Trial*," Max said. "That will give you plenty to live on. Leave the folders to your children. By that time, they can be sold. But tell them, too, that I've stipulated no one can see the material before they bid on it. Tell your daughters they'll get the best price that way. People might be repelled by what the folders reveal and not make an offer. This way the unknown will lead to a bidding frenzy." Really, he had in mind that such a ridiculous restriction might stop anyone from bidding at all. It had become desperately important to Max that the burnt things stay hidden forever, yet he couldn't tell Esther to burn them. No one should ever make that decision. "And remind your children that they're entitled to sell to the highest bidder, even the murderers." Surely the government would stop that, put the whole matter in the courts for some long process that would have made Kafka weep and laugh at once until he choked, which would serve him right.

The stab of anger at someone he still loved made his belly hurt so much he couldn't talk anymore. He heard a horrid high-pitched sound. In his study, someone was cutting through thick bones while the animal was still alive.

17

HE MUST HAVE passed out. When he woke up he was in the hospital again, with tubes coming from his arm. He could still hear the whirring blade, though, and felt like he wanted to vomit his insides onto the floor. "I can't bear this alone," he said.

"I'm here," Esther said, sitting by his bed again.

"Why did he do this to me?" he said.

"The doctor moved you because they can give you stronger narcotics here."

He'd meant to Kafka, of course. That he'd been Kafka's friend had been his greatest honor; more than that, Kafka had been—this was never hidden from Elsa or Esther, or anyone—Max's true love in this life, the only one to whom he'd wanted to be faithful; and this one true love, this Kafka, had betrayed Max by forcing him to betray Kafka, just as Franz had known he would. Thus Max had been faithful to no one, and all so that Kafka could play the egoless, self-denying saint.

It was hard to die feeling like that about Franz, maybe because to lose faith in him was to lose consolation altogether. If Franz's longing for the absolute had been a sham, there wasn't even the possibility that God existed. The universe became infinite, but not as Franz had imagined, as a series of courts within courts that put one off and passed one on, yet let one continue to believe, but as a vast, desolate emptiness that would draw all of Max's particles apart into its silence. It made Max want to scream.

18

MAYBE HE HAD. A middle-aged nurse had appeared with a tray with a hypodermic needle on it. She asked his name, said they had to check each time before administering morphine.

He stared at her in bewilderment. He could have sworn

he'd seen her before, that she should know who he was. That she didn't confused him, made him forget that himself. He looked about the room to find his name, but as he did, he lost other words, like the noun for the role of the woman in the room, or for the brightly colored things in bowls. If he couldn't say who he was, those things wouldn't tell him their names. The world would stare back at him blankly. *He had to remember his own name.*

But before he could find it, the nurse relented, put the tray down on the night table, and picked up the silver needle.

19

HE RAN DOWN A STREET in Tel Aviv, but the city seemed unfamiliar, the buildings older and smaller. He knew he was still chasing a name, but the harder he ran after it, the faster it sprinted ahead of him, like in a fairy tale.

In a doorway ahead a man petted a small lizard with a ridged back. The ridge reminded the running man of his own hump and made him wonder if the people in the windows thought the oddly shaped scurrying creature looked ridiculous. *I need to hide my hump*, he told himself, and—as in a fairy tale—that became a refrain he repeated with each step.

He ran past the doorway, and the man held the lizard

out to him and smiled. The man had perfectly cut finger-nails that reflected the glint of the sun. That sight made the heat today seem pleasant, and he began to walk rather than run. Not having his name began to worry him less, too. In fact, he felt lighter for the loss; after all, the absence of a name gave him the freedom of the city. He could go to a bar if he wanted—not that he did, but he *could*—or to the houses of ill repute, and all without worrying about maintaining his reputation, because he didn't have one anymore. Of course, if no one knew who he was, he might indeed have to go to those low places to buy company for himself.

That prospect made him sad, and he distracted himself with the thought of visiting a restaurant he'd heard about, the sort of place where one could chat with other people who also had barely any name. Franz K. would surely be there.

But wait, wasn't *his* name enormous? No, perhaps not to K., because he had hated it. At that, Max felt again how much he wanted to see him, realized, with a searing poignancy, how much—

20

"HE'S MAX BROD," he heard Esther saying, and he returned to the hospital room, as angry at having been interrupted as a sailor who clung to his desk would be when a sound made the ocean disappear and left him looking ridiculous in a dry room in Prague.

Esther was speaking to another nurse with another tray, a man this time, who must have come in while he'd been away. Probably if the man hadn't gotten that name from Esther, he'd have walked out of the room. Max, though, felt a distaste for the name Esther had used. But what else could he offer the man with the needle instead, so he would give him his drugs? "I'm in pain," he said.

That seemed to satisfy him. He helped Max turn over, lifted the hospital gown, and gave him the injection in his withered buttock.

The nurse shut the door, and Max told Esther that he'd been chasing his own name in Tel Aviv. That sounded like something from a fairy tale. Esther, a practical person, had no use for stories like that, and started to cry.

"No, no, darling, don't worry," Max said. "It was an altogether fine thing, my not having a name." Had it been? "Well, it did mean I'd have to go to a whorehouse. You know what they say, houses of ill repute are for those who have none."

That seemed to make matters worse.

He ignored her. It probably was a fairy tale, or simply nonsense, but it pleased him to think about it more, gave him a moment away from his body, and from this mildly officious woman who was certainly no whore. No, she'd taken him into her bed because Max most certainly did have a name, and even a decent woman wanted one like his. And if the woman wasn't satisfactory, he could, once upon a time, anyway, always find another, and even at the *same* time as the first one, that being what Max desired really, not one faithful Dora Diamant but a crowd of women where he could hide his hump from himself.

The ponderous analyst had seen that well enough, but he'd missed the reason poor Max remained restless: a lover couldn't reassure him that *he* was attractive, because she'd taken his titles into her bed, not the little fellow with the hump. That must be why Franz had come up with his story of "The Poisoned Title." He'd made Max into *Kafka's literary executor*, a name that would feel as stolen as the role of land surveyor, and as hateful as that of Judas; it would be a name Max would hate, even as he used it to earn his living, he'd want to be rid of it to be reduced to a nub of a thing, a letter, a *B*. *That* was why Franz had hung that title round his neck, not for his sainthood but for Max. "The real reason the cat teases the mouse is to prepare him."

That made Esther sob the more. "Franz meant to make me into a character in a story by Franz Kafka," Max said, as if that might stop Esther from crying.

It didn't. She turned away from him, afraid probably that he was raving, or maybe because no woman could ever want a mere B.

But honestly, no, he wasn't that, even here, withered and dying. Franz hadn't seen that he, himself, was the flaw in Kafka's plan (supposing he'd had one). The world's thanks to Max for bravely breaking his promise to Franz meant the poisoned title had led not to infamy but to honor after honor. Max, the brave and much-loved executor of Kafka's estate, had become *Brod*, *Brod* the director of the national theater, *Brod* the composer, *Brod* the author of who can remember how many published books (well, he and Esther could). How could Max think about how *Brod* meant betrayal, when he was surrounded by so many who were grateful for what he'd done? To hate his name in all that admiring din, Max would have had to have been . . . Franz Kafka.

He wasn't. And the one by his bed wasn't Dora Diamant. But having unriddled Kafka's ruse—or probably just having comforted himself with a little Kafka story of his own devising—had given him his Franz again, at least for long enough, he hoped, for Max to finish dying.

He gave Esther's hand a squeeze. She was his sort, really, the kind of woman who knew that titles can be used to overawe even a doctor to obtain a better bed for a Brod. "Like finds like," he said to her.

Esther smiled, as if pleased.

At that, the pain sank its claws into him in earnest, and all stories, whether true or false, disappeared from his mind. He bellowed, and the male nurse came in. Brod said, "It was just playing with me before." He must have sounded mad, and without asking who he was, the man gave him another injection. It transported him

21

to right outside the place he'd wanted, the Tel Aviv restaurant No Soup Today. And under its name on the sign, *nonstop,* though the implication was that it was nonstop not so much because it was service always but service never.

Still, he was glad he'd gone in. Despite its brown walls and simple wooden furniture, it seemed a cheerful place, though something about it also made one think things here were if not actually haphazard, then operating by a different system whose reasons might be as hard to understand as those for the kosher laws. Dora, the chef, could be seen standing in the kitchen, reading a book of Kafka's stories, edited by Max Brod. Dora looked up and waved to him, smiling. "Back to work," she said, but then returned to her reading, not to her stove.

The other diners—and there were quite a few of them—were shouting to the waiter, but in amused rather than angry voices—for now, anyway. After all, no matter how fond they might be of him and the cook, however glad to be in the homeland, still hunger would be a cause of complaint even for the Jews who had been grateful (one might assume) that they'd recently been freed from not having a place, a nation, a name.

Max found himself already seated at a table, looking at a menu that said at the bottom *Not responsible for orders not received* and then added, ominously, *or the ones received.* When he looked up, he saw that his old friend, dressed, as always, in a well-tailored dark suit, was the waiter, which one could tell because he had a white towel draped over his arm.

Max must have looked surprised. "You know what Ben-Gurion wrote," Franz said. "He wanted a country where even the whores and the thieves are Jews, and the writers and luftmenschen are the incompetent waiters."

"You wear a very fine suit for a waiter. You know, I always meant to ask you about those—"

"Luxuries?" Kafka said. "If he does his job dutifully, even the sailor is entitled to his dignity."

"Will there be food?" Brod said nonsensically.

Kafka shrugged. "Probably so. It's a restaurant." He poured Brod some wine. "Here it is nice to give people a drop of wine, because everyone is a little bit of a connoisseur, after all." He spilled a few drops and wiped them up with the towel from his arm, though that meant only that both towel and tablecloth were now stained.

Brod said, "How can I drink if there's no one to pray to Who might bless it?"

Kafka had perhaps become something of a comedian now that he had a homeland—or perhaps because he'd found that even here, he didn't have a homeland. He said, "The trick is to manage the first few sips, Max, then I promise you'll forget about needing Someone to bless it."

Brod drank. The wine was good; sunlight in it, but enough bitterness to keep one tethered to the earth. "Can you drink again, too, Franz?"

Kafka smiled. "There the news is not so good. You must still drink for me, as you did before, in so many different ways." He looked longingly at the wine. "To think that I was once able to manage a big sip of water."

Brod smiled. "So that's why you imagined new clothing?"

"Yes, I couldn't drink it or bathe in it, but perhaps I might at least wear a top hat made of water."

They laughed, and Brod noticed that he was sitting ridiculously in his hospital gown, and maybe because of the wine, or because he was in Franz's presence again, it didn't bother him.

He was glad, in fact, that Esther had appeared at the table to see it. "When I die," Brod said to Kafka, "she'll be in charge of your manuscripts."

"You must burn them," Franz said to her. "Even the burnt things." He poured her some wine.

"I won't," Esther said. "Max loves them too much."

"He does," Kafka said. "You have put it exactly right. Anyone encountering my work after reading his description is bound to be disappointed." He smiled, ironically, even a touch maliciously, and readjusted the towel on his arm. Was the smile at Brod's expense for loving Kafka too much? Or at Franz's own expense, for some more basic mistake, like having even for one moment thought highly of himself?

"Max, Esther may stay awhile longer," Franz said, "but you know that you must now free up that precious bed. You must go into the depths, in the deep harbors."

"Is there a harbor?"

"I was a human being," Franz said.

Did he mean *only* that; so how would I know such things? Or that he'd been a human being, and now he was here, so there was surely more than met the eye to life?

Before he could ask, Franz had adjusted the stained towel over his arm and gone off to take another table's order. Or perhaps to calm some other customers, who, like diners everywhere, were upset over both what has and what hasn't been received.

A LOST STORY
BY FRANZ KAFKA

—AN ODD TITLE, set apart as the first page of a manuscript found among papers in a box in the attic of a pension in Prague. It has no author's name on it, but given, as we'll see, what the owner said about how she'd come by it, it was not unlikely that Franz Kafka himself may have written this story about a man who finds an unpublished story by . . . Franz Kafka.

The story begins when a scholar, long after Kafka's death, had already spent a week in the meager archives in Prague, but had returned each night, disappointed, to the room he'd rented in the attic of a house in a poorer section of Prague. On his way up the stairs, this particular evening, he'd indifferently told the landlady how he'd once again discovered nothing about Kafka that afternoon, nothing new, nothing that might bring him if not fame, at least tenure, and the possibility of the great impossibility for one like him (or he might have added, a little proudly, one like the great Kafka) of an ordinary life, with a wife, and perhaps a child or two. He was careful with his diet, he added almost nonsensically (something about the landlady moved him to speak more personally), but time, nonetheless, was moving on—and seemingly without him.

At that, the landlady, a black-haired gentile, gave him a bold look and a smile, and told him almost proudly that her grandmother had known Kafka, and, she would like to add (for apparently there was something about this thin, wan gentleman that caused her to speak more intimately as well), she had not known him trivially, but *known him* in the very bed the scholar now used.

Kafka, the woman added, had been quite the lover—the remark showing (for please remember that you are here, we imagine, reading a story by Kafka) that the supposedly retiring author was not without his vanity in this matter. The full-bosomed woman gave a wink, and even a leer that the scholar (who was not very familiar with female desire) couldn't forget on his way up the stairs, perhaps because, as he noted to himself, it was exactly the sort of thing Kafka found attractive—at least in his women characters.

He stopped on the second landing, a little short of breath, and thought that one might be hard-pressed to say that his landlady's "quite" hadn't been, in fact, her way of saying *odd*, which interpretation would mean that as a lover Kafka wasn't a man mighty in appetite but perhaps one more like the Kafka who chewed each mouthful of meat precisely three hundred times before swallowing, supposedly for health, but really (who would know better than the author) because of a self-imposed kosher law that made any meal a difficulty for himself and a source of disgust to others. The scholar could only imagine the equivalent laws that he obeyed in bed, even (he's resumed climbing; he's arrived in the room and thrown himself down to rest) this wonderfully and improbably soft feather bed.

Perhaps the large-breasted woman noted the scholar's avidity for her story. The next morning she came to his attic room in her dressing gown, and, seemingly without a thought for the proprieties, sat on the edge of the bed where he still lay under bedclothes that were much nicer than one had a right to expect in such a shabby house. The scholar felt unsure as to what the exact nature of this encounter was to be—until he saw in her hand some yellowing, badly smudged manuscript pages that were, she said, one of her family's most precious possessions (though that hardly would account for how haphazardly, even carelessly, the supposed treasure had been treated). The pages, she said, were a story of Franz Kafka's.

It is hard to explain how eager the man was to see the story, though perhaps, for our purposes, the most appropriate analogy would be that the story was to him like a tethered animal to a hungry wolf. Perhaps some of that avidity on his part also flowed over the story and onto the woman in whose hand it rested. Still, he snatched it from her and began to read even before she had left the room to make his breakfast.

This story within a story within a bedroom may seem very odd to you, and almost make you doubt its authenticity—but perhaps not so very odd if it's by the same author who, without any explanation, turned a man into a dung beetle, and imagined an art that consisted of starving one's self to death. And the handwriting—ah, if only one had a chance to look at the actual manuscript, which would be in a spidery scrawl, a design that looked so very much like the patterns traced by the harrow of the penal-colony torture device—well, really, even if it hadn't been so much what the scholar desired, he, at least, would have no doubt that he had found a lost story by Franz Kafka.

One which began by reminding the reader of the familiar, though always terrifying, Bible verses about Abraham and Isaac, the father whose much-loved son had been the gift the patriarch had been promised by God for his faithfulness, though it was not, such is God's way with time (as the Jews who await their messiah, or the Christians who await his return), a promise that the Lord seemed to have been in any rush to fulfill. Fortunately, Abraham always took great care with his diet (immediately this odd chiming translated the scholar into the story within a story; he saw himself as the father of the Jews); he ate no meat, for example, and was still hale at a hundred years old when God had gotten around to him, and his son had been born, the first of those many descendants who God had promised him would someday be more numerous than the stars. Abraham had trusted in God; God had kept faith with him. Now God had said he must kill this very son.

He delayed only long enough to sharpen his knife (and he so wanted to delay, and so wanted his son's end both never to come and to be painless and quick when it did, that you can imagine how long he worked and how sharp he must have made that knife); he packed wood for the offering and left immediately, not telling anyone why he must make this trip. Truly, he didn't know *why*, could not understand this monstrous demand. But he had to trust God's murderous guidance, and if he did—he looked up at the night sky for reassurance—God, perhaps, would (in time!) keep faith with him again.

Fire made. Child bound to the rocks. Then, at the last instant, as his knife was poised over his son's throat, God had relented. Had it all been a test whose right answer was that if Abraham so trusted God that he would kill his own son, then he didn't have to kill his son, but could—as God now commanded—kill the goat that the Lord had made conveniently available, tangled in a thicket nearby?

Of course, since Adam was cast from the Garden, there was never a time when the animals could talk; but in Abraham's time, one closer to Eden, they were far more expressive, and could make their feelings, and even their thoughts, known to men. The goat used its eyes—so haunting and lovely, with an air of sad bewilderment, however goatish his actions had been in the past—to plead for its life. He offered promises—but what can a goat promise compared to God? and he flattered Abraham, who was, he said, a good man, one who never ate meat—cleverly adding (to show his sincerity) that that goodness persisted even if Abraham followed that diet only because he thought it was healthier. Surely, here, as always, Abraham had done (the goat conveyed) what God wanted all men to do. Hadn't God once, in the time before Noah, already drowned the world because men weren't satisfied with the bountiful fruits and cereals He'd offered them for their food, and had fallen ravenously on the animals? Which *must* mean that God wanted us to spare His creatures, and by simple logic, must want Abraham to spare him.

All this the animal spoke with its eyes, and with the panting panic of his heaving chest, the quiver in his legs, the slight turns of his body (though he could hardly move,

Abraham's knife was pressed so close to the veins in his neck).

Abraham remembered that he, too, had heard of that first flood, God discarding the grand labor of the six days because men had eaten meat. But had God destroyed the world because men killed animals (in which case, he should spare the expressive goat), or because they had disobeyed Him (in which case he should do as God had ordered him and kill the wily goat)? Abraham couldn't decide. This, too, might be another test, just like the command to kill his son. But what was the right answer? The goat's pleading was driving him mad, and trembling with fury with the goat (or was it with God?) for putting him in this quandary, his arm moved ever so slightly, almost haphazardly, and sliced the thick but delicate vein in the goat's neck, a shallow cut that nonetheless could not ever be taken back, one that was so small that it caused the animal's blood to drain slowly, though inevitably and irretrievably, onto the desert floor. But worse than the blood, if such a thing's possible, was the last look of disappointment, of bewilderment made infinite, that the kid gave him as its life trickled away.

Abraham was certain he'd made a mistake. He stood still, head bowed, and waited for the divine knife that would cut his throat. But God did not punish him. If there had been a test, perhaps he'd passed.

Abraham, as the goat had said, had never eaten meat, but not out of goodness, or even, truly, for health. He simply didn't care for its taste, which smelt rotten in his nose. Now it all the more reminded him of death and, worse, his own murderous impulses; the odor made him sick to his stomach. But he knew he must not betray that he'd ever had doubts, that he'd nearly not fulfilled God's command to him. So he ate meat at every meal to show God that the blood of animals meant nothing to him. Chewed it thoroughly to show that this horrifying thing didn't horrify him (or perhaps the repeated motion leached some of the horror out of the flesh for him, made it possible to swallow and digest this carrion thing). Alas, each bite, each working of jaw and mandible, reminded him of the goat's eyes, the goat's blood, his own confusion, his haphazard violence— and, most of all, his near mistake when he'd almost been won over by the devilish goat into disobeying God.

Worse still, Abraham knew he hadn't meant to kill the goat, that he hadn't been truly obedient, and he suspected, too, that his hiding of his real feelings (bite by bite) toward the goat was to pile error on error. At any moment, God would punish him. Perhaps, in fact, this continual nausea was punishment, though only a first installment of the final pain he'd feel. (Where? In his neck? In his heart?) Or maybe he was being punished like this because God had wanted him to spare the goat?

It may be that eating meat didn't shorten Abraham's life (though, again, perhaps it did), but it did make every meal a misery to him—and equally wearying to those who happened to eat *with* him, most particularly for Isaac, his beloved son, a child of delicate digestion. Perhaps because of those awful meals with his father—for God's sake, three hundred grindings of teeth before he would swallow a bite—this dyspepsia was handed down from generation to generation of the Jews—

Until Moses, who understood what had happened to Abraham (and then to Isaac, Jacob, and Joseph, and their progeny more numerous than the stars). In order to justify the Patriarch, and perhaps ease everyone's burden, Moses, without divine sanction, turned the goat's slow bleeding into a Law, hoping this might restore his people's appetite.

Of course God was horrified that a man, even Moses, would meddle with his intricately calibrated Torah—condemning His animals to lingering deaths. But He, in his wisdom, didn't want to call this human and invented law into question, lest people begin to pick and choose among the other mitzvahs, saying maybe some of them had been added on by men as well. He didn't correct the text, but punished Moses for this transgression by barring him from entering the promised land.

So the story ended. Or did it? A scholar who found this parable would know, of course, that Kafka had told his friend Brod to destroy all his work upon his death. Surely, though, that must mean only the known work? After all, this lost story could make the scholar's reputation, and though, from the quality of the parable, he might doubt that the story would add much to Kafka's luster, he might hope it wouldn't detract much, either.

Should he publish? What would Kafka want done? Hadn't he really just told Brod to burn his work in order to make Brod into what he'd most wanted to be, a divided ever-miserable character in a story by the genius he most admired, Franz Kafka? And if this man were a true scholar, then that would be how he, too, felt about himself and his author—that his life was a story narrated by Kafka.

And if Kafka had written *this* story, in which a man is visiting Prague because of his work, it would seem to indicate that he'd imagined that whatever he'd intended, he at least suspected that Brod might not obey him, and that he would be famous long after his death.

Would the scholar, as he himself suspected, be saying all this only to justify his publishing the story, getting tenure, and so being able to do what Kafka had never done, which was to marry his beloved? Even if the scholar didn't eat meat, he might be said to have a good appetite, so he didn't make meals a misery for the other guests at this pension. Why shouldn't such a man marry? Perhaps even the woman who had rented him this low-ceilinged room with the comfortable well-stuffed bed, this grandchild of Kafka's lover, whose ample bosom, and open, even wanton, sexual look he would have found he couldn't bar from his dreams. Perhaps he could have her here, in this bed that she had said had been blessed by Kafka, the two of them lost in feathers.

But not tonight. The confusions around and in this story would give a man a stomachache.

Of course, he would publish the story and be recommended for tenure. And marry. But a man who'd found a new parable by Kafka would also discover that all the questions posed in it—which are really one question: What does God really want from us?—had taken up residence in his body. But, far worse, he would see from the way his own children walked, always as if a wind buffeted them from side to side, that he'd burdened them with the same worries, the same ambivalence, whose result would be that one felt that a world so insecurely both held and pushed away might be snatched from you at any moment. Or perhaps he gave them that fatal gift not because of a story but because that would have been the kind of person he always would have been, whether he had found a lost story or not, and maybe that "gift"—which is to say, his personality— would have been what had first attracted him to the study of Kafka, in whose work he might see his flaws made even worse, and yet at the same time transformed into art.

Whatever the reason was for what had happened to his children, burdening one's progeny does not answer a question of whether (for example) God wanted the goat to die. To know the answer to that is perhaps the way to the true promised land. But like Moses, he and his children were barred from that.

Fortunately, and though a scholar's once healthy wife surely would lose her own appetite from the contagion of eating and sleeping alongside him, and though the children have found themselves so divided in heart, not everyone feels crushed by questions. In Kafka's other stories, the burdened and so burdensome characters will most likely die, and perhaps this scholar will choke to death at his dinner this very evening. (Dear God, Max, even I was surprised when I wrote that, shocked at how easily an author stops his character's throat when he can barely get any water down his own anymore. It seems one is both executioner and goat—a worn insight, and one which I can assure you does not lead to the promised land.) But after a disaster, to mock the melancholy character, or to give the reader hope, Kafka often also ends his stories with a vision of health. After Gregor Samsa's corpse is swept into the trash, his sister, freed finally from feeding and caring for him (however halfheartedly and disgustedly), extends her body in a gesture of youth and joy; and next to the cage where the emaciated corpse of the Hunger Artist lies forgotten in the hay, the sideshow customers stare avidly through the bars of the prison next door at a beautiful pacing leopard. So at the end of this story, please remember that many will sit down happily tonight to a well-cooked meal, will eat their meat with good appetite, and—mercifully for their families—quickly, too. And they'll drink, too, without giving it a thought. After all, Max, as I once told you, when we sat together on that bench one gray Prague day, "There's plenty of hope, an infinite amount of hope," and plenty of meat and air, too, I might have added. Though I admit, I also said, "but not for

and here the manuscript breaks off.

LUSK AND MARIANNE

1

AT THE BEGINNING OF 1931, the Communist Party of Germany tasked Ludwig (Lusk) Lask, a twenty-five-year-old course trainer for the Marxist Workers Evening School, with teaching the rudiments of economics to the members of the Brandenburg-Berlin Agitprop Department. Unfortunately, the party office had given Lusk the address for the apartment building where he was to hold the class, and the party name of the cadre, but not the flat number or the member's real name, which would, of course, be the one on the door.

This made Lusk smile wryly, but in no way diminished his faith in the Communist Party of Germany. Not that he was a naïf. Far from it. His mother, the famous playwright Bertha Lask, was a party member, as was his brother, Hermann. His mother knew the leadership, and they often came to dinner at his family's house, along with fellow travelers such as the great cynic Bertolt Brecht; the party's petty internal politics provided Lusk's family's table talk. But those squabbles, Lusk knew, were like a play of foam above waves; the ocean was the proletariat, and Lenin, who his mother called the party's "animating and protecting spirit," was, he supposed, none other than the Man in the Moon, who guided the ocean's tides.

Lusk wholeheartedly shared his mother's admiration for Lenin; he'd learned Russian at sixteen to read him in his original language, and to make himself someone the party might choose for membership. And in the story Lusk narrated to himself this suburban night, "Lusk Lask, a thin wiry, long-legged fellow, whose coat wasn't warm enough for a late fall night, walked with strong, confident strides through the suburban streets of Zehlendorf because he was being used by the leadership of the Leninist Party, the only force that could defeat fascism and make a world of brotherhood." Still, his faith in the party might have been still greater if someone in the office had given him the real name of the woman who rented the apartment where he was to teach.

Fortunately, when he got to the building, he found he could see through the street-level windows to a flat where people had spread out on couches, on folding seats, and on the floor. They spoke loudly, and made broad—yes, theatrical—gestures. Lusk compared them to the workers he usually taught, comrades who had a sincere, determined air made up of both confidence and resignation; they made clear that they might not like what was thrown at them by the bosses, but they would do whatever was necessary to survive and move forward. After all, what choice did they have?

He stepped behind a table set up for him at the front of the room and began the course by describing the one class that, if it didn't receive the party's correctives, was most likely to produce work that they might think revolutionary, but that would really serve the rulers. This was, of course, the class into which he, and probably many of the people here, had been born, the petit bourgeoisie. Lenin, fortunately, had given all of them a way to guard against this self-deception; cadre must accept party discipline and let the party ruthlessly unmask and correct them when they found themselves clinging to imaginary distinctions, such as a degree in philosophy, a place in the theater, a small shop, or whatever.

The workers in his classes had been attentive, like prisoners who believed Marx knew the way out of their jail. The actors, on the other hand, looked mocking. As always when he doubted himself, Lusk began to feel hollow, like a papier-mâché figure which might tip over at any time. To steady himself, his gaze returned to a small, attractive, full-breasted woman with a light blue shawl around her shoulders. She had large, sympathetic eyes that told him she both believed he'd something valuable to say and was sorry for the difficulty her comrades had made for him in saying it. But she looked so sad to him, he found he wanted to comfort *her*, tell her things weren't really that bad.

As soon as he finished, he moved toward her and stumbled over a thick white cast on a man's leg, making himself look both foolish and inconsiderate. The woman, it turned out, was the Dora Diamant whose name had been on the front door, and she was also the party's *Maira Jalens*. And the large-eared man he'd tripped over to get to her was, she said proudly, not only an actor but a brave Yiddish playwright. Three Brownshirts had followed him home after their last performance; two had held him while the third had swung a bat that broke his left leg, below the knee.

Lusk winced. Six feet tall, he himself had long, sinewy legs of which he was a little proud, and just before he'd stumbled, he'd been hoping that Dora would notice them when he came toward her.

Soon others came up to talk to Dora, some of them, Lusk saw now, also bruised. Dora had the same respectful, sympathetic attitude toward all of them that she had for Lusk. Strangely, though that made him jealous, it didn't diminish his sense of its value when her kindness was directed toward him.

After each class, he pushed forward through the men and women around Dora and made sure they got to talk together. She told him that she was the widow of Franz Kafka, but that name didn't mean anything to Lusk. A writer, she added reverently. Lusk imagined that like Dora, Kafka's work would be socially and politically aware, though Dora spoke less about the politics of her own work as an actress, and more about "a gesture's emotional truth," which meant something different from realism, something about the expressive hand being moved by some unseen power (and not, from the sound of it, either the proletariat or the capitalist market). Lusk didn't see what she meant, and suspected it was foolishness, but he could see that she had an inner radiance, and a generosity that attracted others—making her like his own mother in that way. There was, also like his mother, an air of inaccessibility to Dora. She liked Lusk, or so he thought, but he didn't feel she in any way required him. She had a sense of completeness about her.

He told her that last part, and, sadly for Lusk, she credited her husband for it. He'd died seven years before, after such a small time together, but he'd given her so many things, she said, a lifetime of riches (was she boasting, or giving him a warning?), including the inspiration for her career. She and this tubercular man had read to each other in their little apartment—a place not far from here—and that had been her first encounter with Kleist, Heine, Ibsen, even Goethe. Her lover had said her recitations had great purity, and had encouraged her to become an actress, and his words, or so Lusk felt, had had for Dora the force of a dying man's wishes.

And she'd become a powerful actress, Brecht said at dinner that week. "Which is all the worse for anything she's in, as she is effective in a dreadful style, all hand on heart, *Oh, Schmerz! Schmerz!*"

Lusk remembered his first talk to the agitprop group, his sense that she felt too worried for him. Had she been acting? But why? If it was because she had found him attractive, that might be even better than if she'd felt concerned for him.

"It's a dangerous style for Agitprop," Brecht said. "The time I saw her, everyone wept for and with this woman,"

Brecht said, "and while they did, the Brownshirts arrived, and they all finished by weeping for themselves."

"And you?" Isaac Chazzan asked. He was the Yiddish playwright whose cast Lusk had tripped over. He had a smile that was ironic but also accepting, almost fond. "I know you must have fought back against the SA manfully, with fists and sticks."

Brecht, who was famously the great coward, smiled back—equally accepting, but of himself. "Still, one has to make do," he said, referring not to the physically craven Brecht—the only Brecht we have, after all—but to his own struggles with actors. "The Dora I remember is certainly pretty, Lusk. Slight and short, no? Yet with such large breasts. Seemingly gentle, too, but who knows what's behind all that *Schmerz*. Something very steely and self-possessed, I'll bet." Brecht, who made such a point of displaying his appetites that one doubted how much pleasure they truly gave him, made it clear that he wouldn't mind fucking her. Of course, he probably wouldn't have minded fucking Lusk, too, or Lusk's mother. It wasn't much of an honor to be desired by the bullet-faced great seducer.

Lusk felt how much he wanted to protect Dora from Brecht's gross appetites, or from the SA, or from whatever dangers history might threaten her with. This adolescent attitude was, he knew, both condescending and petty bourgeois of him, and called for rigorous self-examination. After all, without it, cadre that formed into couples might try to protect each other at a demonstration, at a time when there should be no room for personal concerns as to who took a beating or who had the chance to hand one out. Party cadre had to place themselves beyond affections, beyond good and evil even, and fight with whatever sacrifice and brutality the Party deemed necessary, so they might make a world where brutality and sacrifice would no longer be necessary.

Lusk reassured himself that he would always put the necessary discipline first, and after the next class he waited till most of the others had left, then made his way to Dora. She thanked him for the evening's lecture and called him "a servant of the Incorruptible."

He felt flattered but a little confused. It turned out that the Incorruptible (he had the feeling from her tone that the word should be capitalized) was something that people often knew in love, or sometimes through a belief in God. Her late husband, though, had given her an idea that it might be in other things, as well. Lusk came from the party of the working class, and he expounded the truth of History, so that made him an agent of the Incorruptible.

Not long ago, this very transcendence of self into *agent* had been all Lusk wanted. Now he resented that he didn't have something more intimate and personal to offer her, something *in particular*. Which once again showed that the party had been right. Cadre shouldn't form couples. It kept one from having a Communist attitude.

Her dead husband stared down at them from a silver-framed picture on the mantelpiece. He looked terrified.

"What large eyes, he has," Lusk said, in what he hoped was a neutral tone. *And what* huge *ears,* he might have added.

Perhaps she thought he'd meant how piercing the Kafka gaze, how far-seeing. Perhaps his praising him pleased her. In any case, Lusk and Dora made love for the first time that night, and Lusk's own sharp eyes went happily blind.

Usually, the sensual world evaded or bored Lusk unless he could give it some world-historical significance, but in the days that followed he loved simply, and without thinking, to kiss the nape of Dora's neck, to watch the way she gestured with her small hands, and, most of all, to feel those hands touching him *in particular*. He decided sex with Dora meant transcending himself and most being himself at once; and then he stopped thinking about that, too, and felt her lips on his, the press of her breasts against his chest, her hands touching his legs. Ludwig (Lusk) Lask, he narrated to himself, was in love.

Which made him all the more vulnerable to the pain Herr Ears could cause him. Every word about Kafka (and it seemed as though Dora's mouth released flocks of them every day) hurt like a sharp peck to his body. And it wasn't just words; Dora's Kafka Museum had objects in it, too, such as the picture, or a fountain pen or even a hairbrush of his. He loathed those things, and even more that she sometimes got small royalty payments from his estate.

"Don't be foolish," his mother said. "She needs the money to live on, so she can struggle for the rights of the proletariat." Bertha thought her son too much troubled by a ghost.

This ghost, however, was very real to Dora, perhaps because when alive, the writer had himself foolishly believed in ghosts. He'd made her burn his manuscripts, for example, to ward off the unseen presences.

"Her feelings about this man will change," his mother said. "That is, if you want her enough to give her a child. When you do that, the phantom will disappear like so much mist."

Soon Dora petitioned the party to change her membership to his cell, and she moved in with him at his parents' house. She still performed with her agitprop troop, but on her free days she worked with Lusk to produce the party newspaper (his newly assigned task) and sell it at meetings. Dora might not yet belong altogether to Lusk, but she'd given herself wholly to the party, to the work against Hitler, and to the pleasures of the Lusks' home, the books everywhere, the burnished wood, the warmth of Lusk's father (a cultured and famous neurologist), the fierce debates at the dinner table.

And that life together also gave Lusk many opportunities to eavesdrop. "It was the same when he prepared tea for a visitor," he heard Dora saying to his mother one morning, and he stopped outside the kitchen door to listen. "When Franz performed even a simple, seemingly insignificant action like that," she said, "he made it seem as if he were doing it for someone that he revered."

His mother, from the sound of it, must be making Dora some tea—though apparently with an inferior, only human level of concentration.

"His manner gave everything he did a religious intensity," Dora said, and Lusk could easily imagine her infuriating fond smile. "Of course, this thoroughness kept him so busy that he didn't manage to put the cup of tea on the table. He used up all his strength in the preparation."

His mother placed something that sounded solid on the round glass table in the alcove off the kitchen. "Then there was no tea, Dora?" his mother said. "Was it Kafka's concern that friends were supposed to drink? You make me wonder if the man had ever been thirsty."

At that, Dora had run through the swinging door and right past Lusk. She said nothing about his spying, just rushed on toward their bedroom, weeping. Apparently, no one but Kafka had ever known what thirst truly meant.

Lusk decided to learn all he could about his rival. He read *The Trial*—unfinished—and *The Castle,* also unfinished, both of them stories about and by a petit-bourgeois defeatist who couldn't even manage to give his character a name. They showed no social and political awareness.

Lusk told her that as he and Dora leafleted on Unter den Linden. She said nothing, and handed a man in a cloth cap a leaflet for their last big rally before the vote, and smiled at him, but the man didn't look at that lovely gesture in his rush to get to a warmer place. Lusk, overcome by love, decided he must get Dora a better coat.

Their post was near the university, a place busy with a mix of students, bourgeois, workers, yet as everyone rushed by, their faces set against leaflets and cold, Dora said she felt as though it wasn't the German working class against Hitler anymore, only the two of them.

He reassured her that the party had posted many other

teams up and down the avenue, and, in any case, a Communist should always know he's not alone; he's part of the masses in motion.

But what if a Communist *wanted*, if only occasionally, to be alone with his wife? How could he do that as long as a ghost was always with them, too? Lusk had to reduce the writer in size so he could blow him away. He told Dora that *The Trial* was meant to convince the petite bourgeoisie that one needn't take up the struggle for justice; a man was an isolated atom, and all struggles end in defeat.

Dora, oddly, agreed. Joseph K's struggle was futile, but Lusk didn't understand why. In fact, no one who hadn't known Franz could understand him.

"That will certainly limit his readership."

She ignored that. "Franz condemns Joseph K. because he tries to shape his life differently from the life of crucifixion, the only life there is."

Dora, he wanted to say—to cry, perhaps, as if from the cross—if you think there's no life but crucifixion, what do you think we're doing here handing out leaflets? What are we struggling for?

"You can hold back from the suffering of the world," Dora said, "but perhaps this holding back is the one suffering you could have avoided."

He could tell from her tone that she was quoting *him*, and wondered why the phrases didn't make his ears bleed. Before he could reply, one of the Nazi trucks came by, with Hitler's voice blaring from a gramophone record. Dora watched it pass. "Sometimes," she said, "I feel like we're on horseback." She meant, he knew, that Hitler had a private plane, and traveled to fifteen well-staged rallies each day.

The party had many brave horse cavalry—handing out leaflets—but they were charging the machine guns of the twentieth century.

"No," Lusk said, against all the mechanical evidence, "the Nazis are the ones in costumes from the past. Only the proletariat can give birth to the future."

And Hindenburg won the runoff. He banned the SA while he investigated the accusation that they'd plotted a coup. That made for a momentary lull in the street fighting, and a chance for the agitprop troop to work again. "But what does it mean about us," his brother Hermann asked at dinner, "that the midwife of the future depends for its survival on that remnant of feudalism?"

Still, it relieved the pressure on all their chests a little, gave them a chance to work more freely. And it even let Lusk go so far as to have a drink with a comrade who had brought someone that he said Lusk had to meet—a Joseph Polack, whose former wife had had an affair with the very man Lusk himself seemed always to be talking about, the writer Franz Kafka.

This fellow, Polak, was a square-faced Jew with a monocle. It saddened Lusk that despite the silly eyepiece, Polak was handsome; if Kafka might have an affair with this man's wife, then perhaps the picture in the silver frame didn't do him justice.

But then, it hadn't precisely been an affair, Polak said, only a grand epistolary romance, "a *white* passion, if you believe in such a thing." Polak thought Kafka had gone to whores in Prague, but he believed Franz couldn't have an erection with Milena. "Maybe it was because, as Milena said, that he hated the flesh, maybe it was because she was a gentile, and Franz hated himself."

People stared at them. Had they heard the fool talk about a Jew fucking a gentile?

Polak gulped his beer and gestured peremptorily for the sullen waiter—a stupid way to act in combustible Berlin—certain of the aggrieved waiter's obedience and of Lusk's wallet.

"Franz was maybe not much of a lover," he said, and his voice lost a bit of his overdone bonhomie, "but he *was* a great writer, and, I'll tell you, a very heroic person." He let the monocle drop out of his eye and acted as if he reflected inwardly. "He truly couldn't tell a lie, and he was, at every moment, engaged in a great trial of conscience, a truly extraordinary monologue directed toward a God Franz didn't believe was listening."

To Lask, that part of the report sounded like praise for the ridiculous—a mad man shouting and gesticulating at an emptiness—but the rest might contain a kernel of comfort for him, and the next night, when he and Dora were in bed, Lusk told her about the meeting with the monocle-wearing Jew.

"I know all about Milena," Dora said flatly.

"He said Milena told him Kafka feared the flesh." Foolish thing to say; what if she replied, *But not my flesh?*

Dora sat up. The sheet dropped from her breasts. "I think, Lusk, what you really want to ask is, did Franz put his penis in my vagina?" She stared at him in a way both furious and vulnerable, and Lusk felt mortified at the transformation he'd caused in this unfailingly gentle woman.

Dora, in turn, must have seen his stricken look. She touched his hair, told him that she loved him, and that he, Ludwig (Lusk) Lask, was her life now. She spoke for the first time of their having a child.

Lusk, pleased and terrified (a child—a Jewish child? and today, when a million German voices spoke of murdering Jews?), was still almost jealous enough to ask if Kafka would have approved. But that would have been foolish. Really, would Dora have said it if Kafka *hadn't* approved?

Besides, what did that matter? Kafka was in the ground in Prague, Lusk was in bed with Dora in Berlin. *You will give her a child,* his mother had said, *and her Kafka will disappear.* Well, they would see now, wouldn't they?

If they survived. By the time of the next election for deputies, the SA had been reinstated, and had soon doubled its number. The party assigned as many men as they could to protect the agitprop performances, but every show had ended in a battle, and when one of his comrades took out a Luger, Lusk confessed (or boasted) to the dinner guests that he'd felt the weight of the pistol in his own hands, and the feel of the trigger the man had pulled that had made blood bloom on a brown shirt. The Nazi's scream made him feel there was nothing contingent in his life; all had been fated, and even as they'd run from the SS, Lusk had never more felt the master. He'd positively wanted to bellow in triumph from the exultation of it all.

To which Dora said nothing, only looked down at her plate. Lusk had wanted it all to mean *I'm not like Kafka,* but he'd probably only made himself look ridiculous.

"The problem isn't my brother's bloodlust," Hermann

said. "It's that the tally of wounded is the wrong way round. The party thinks our real enemy is the Social Democrats."

"Hermann's right," the great prophet Brecht said. "The Social Democrats think Hitler's stupid but useful. They believe he'll destroy the Communists for them, and they'll take over. The Comintern thinks, Let's get rid of the Social Democrats, even if it brings Hitler to power. The vagabond will fail to save capitalism, and we'll take over. Hitler, though, he knows that in gross times, it's better to consider things in a cruder way. He thinks, I have three hundred thousand Storm Troopers. As soon as I take over, I'll murder every Social Democrat and Communist left alive."

Lusk's mother said, "Hitler's outvoted in the Reichstag and in the cabinet. We'll force new elections. He won't be chancellor anymore by June."

"Or we'll all be dead by then," Brecht said.

"Don't be foolish," Lusk's mother replied, and the other guests listened most attentively to her. Bertha Lask had buried two brothers in the war, and had written a great pacifist play, but that had only brought her a despair that hadn't dissipated until she'd embraced Lenin, and the need for a violence to end violence. Her reluctant journey gave her commitments an imperative force. People made wry faces at Brecht's aphorisms, but they rested themselves in Lusk's mother's reassurance and returned to their fish—except, that is, for Dora, of course, who, like her former husband, was a vegetarian.

On the thirtieth of January, when elections had achieved only stalemates, the senile Hindenburg appointed Adolf Hitler chancellor. On the twenty-seventh of February, the

Nazis staged their own bit of epic theater. They burnt the Reichstag and hung a Communist for starting the fire. All but the party's own parliamentary delegates voted Hitler emergency powers. "The German people long to do away with their own will," Dora said to him in bed that night. "They want to pledge obedience to a vengeful god."

That evening, the great playwright Bertolt Brecht fled Germany.

Soon after, the opposition newspapers had their presses destroyed, their staff arrested. The SA shuttered all trade union offices, arrested the officers, and put them in camps. In May, they took away the prominent Communists, including Lusk's mother.

They also seized some manuscripts, including a notebook of Kafka's aphorisms that Dora must have hidden from the implacable invalid by some sleight of hand when he'd ordered her to burn his things. Dora was inconsolable—for the manuscripts, in Lusk's opinion, not for Bertha, though Lusk would have said she liked his mother very much. There were many mothers, he supposed, but only one copy of Kafka's aphorisms in the world.

Without her permission, Lusk had already read them one night, months before, the manuscript no more than eighty pages, with only one or two sentences to a page, as if Kafka thought his words were holy writ. Much speculation about God—always present, but dangerous if ever named—many warnings against collaboration with the demons. *The reservations with which you take Evil into yourself are not yours, but those of Evil.* Et cetera.

He couldn't see the use, but to comfort Dora, he said,

"They were good. Piercing, even." Of course that might make the loss worse. Or she might say, *How dare you have touched Franz's things.*

But she seemed pleased. They were united for a moment, so he didn't add, *A lot of them I couldn't understand.* After all, no one could who hadn't known Franz. On the other hand, he was beginning to feel that he had known him, and all too well.

After three weeks, his mother had been released from a basement near the university with much of her beautiful black hair gone, and some of it turned white. "The Jews," Bertha said, "don't believe in hell. But we're wrong. It's right below the houses of Berlin." Beyond that, she wouldn't say what had happened to her.

Within the month Lusk's sister, her husband, and her child had left for Holland, and his parents and his brothers had fled Prague to wait for permission—granted only to the most loyal party members—to enter the Soviet Union. The party, though, had tasked Ludwig Lask with the production and distribution of the now-illegal newspaper in the Steglitz area. Dora was a few weeks pregnant but decided to stay and work with him, moving from apartment to apartment every few weeks as a safety measure.

An ineffective one. At the beginning of August, the Gestapo came for Ludwig (Lusk) Lask.

Lusk had been taken to a wooden barracks and tortured for weeks with barbed wire wrapped on a stick. He screamed from the pain, but, as the party had instructed, he denied any involvement in Communism. He listened to the sounds of executions and was told he'd be next if he didn't provide information on his comrades. Lusk pissed himself but remained faithful to the leadership's directive and denied he had any comrades.

And the party's wisdom had once again been his salvation. The Gestapo decided that "Ludwig Lask had no information about plans hostile to the state" and, though a Jew, was not a Communist. They released him.

Lusk had done the hardest thing in his life; he'd kept his integrity, had betrayed no one. His spouse, however, had been disloyal to him, and had named their two-week-old child Franziska Marianne, in honor of the one forever Incorruptible thing in her life. His usually discerning mother, Lusk thought, had been wrong: Dora Diamant Kafka would never truly become Ludwig Lask's wife.

But when he held his daughter, his Marianne, his anger was replaced by a compound of love and terror for his infant much stronger than he'd expected, much stronger than anything he'd thought himself capable of feeling. The touch of her skin overcame his isolation, gave him a connection to a wider view, in which he felt himself not reduced but almost infinitely extended. He put his thumb in her small, soft palm and wished only that her fingers might one day curl around his.

He believed Dora loved him, at least a little, but she would never need him. His fragile infant daughter, by contrast, required his protection at every moment, and his help in learning about the world. He could teach her scientific Marxism-Leninism instead of self-defeating aphorisms.

If Lusk's mother could play on her ties with the German party leadership in exile and get permission for the new family to join her, Marianne would even have the great privilege of growing up in the first Workers' State, where his daughter could solve the difficult technical problems of building industry that served humanity, rather than endlessly stumbling over the pointless, insoluble contradictions of an absent God.

And if his mother couldn't get them visas, she and her parents would almost certainly be hunted down by the Nazis and murdered.

II

1

ALMOST AS SOON as the Lasks came together in Moscow, they would have to part again, Hermann for a construction project at the Stalingrad Tractor Factory, and his parents for Sebastopol, where his father would take up his research again, but now in service to all humanity. He, Dora, and Marianne had to remain in the city, where Lusk had been given a job as a researcher at the Marxist-Leninist Institute (and membership in the Soviet Communist Party) and where Dora, if the Soviet party agreed to transfer her membership from the KPD, might find work in the Yiddish theater.

Tonight would be their last dinner together for a long while, and they chose a restaurant with plush red carpets, white tablecloths, and meat on the menu, a place favored by party officials. Lusk took pleasure in the way the waiter refilled their crystal water glasses—efficient without being obsequious—but what one felt from the officials' burdened faces, and the bottles of vodka on the tables, wasn't privilege and pleasure but a sense of foreboding and grim resolve. As the papers said, the rapid march to industrialization had been bound to intensify class divisions, and that week Zinovyev and Kamenev had confessed in open court that at Trotsky's order, they'd arranged for Kirov's assassination.

Dora, like a child who needed the multiplication table explained over and over, had asked, "But why did Trotsky want to have Kirov killed?"

Hermann said, "For the same reason that the KPD would burn down the Reichstag."

"But we didn't burn down the Reichstag."

Hermann gave a twisted smile. Lusk did not. This wasn't a laughing matter. The conspiracies of Trotskyites, working hand in glove with the Western powers, were much more dangerous and widespread than his brother suspected. The NKVD had even uncovered deviationists within his own Marxist-Leninist Institute, including the deputy head, Jan Sten, who'd once been one of Stalin's tutors on Hegel.

His mother looked around the room, said, "Enough politics, let's talk about something else." No doubt, she didn't want her family fighting in a way that might disturb the leadership.

Chocked by new sorrows, Lusk soon forgot about the Trotskyites. His two-year-old daughter had scarlet fever, and the cost of the Soviet Union's rapid industrialization had left the Soviet state no international credits with which to buy penicillin. They had one hope, though: Lusk had to stay in Moscow, but Dora could take Marianne to his parents' house in Sebastopol, where the weather itself, his father said, might work a cure.

It would be two months before Lusk could get permission to visit Sebastopol again, and when he walked across the lawn toward his daughter, she hid herself from the strange man behind her grandfather's leg. When Lusk tried to kiss her, she turned her head downward, and his lips only touched her hair. He could feel himself disappear.

On the bureau in Dora's room, he found the picture of Kafka, a solvent that ate away more of Lusk's presence in the world. Next to the silver frame, his wife had left the first page of the account of her life that she had to write so she could transfer her membership to the Soviet party. It began, *I married the German-Czech writer Dr. Franz Kafka, who then died in the year 1924.*

He turned on her furiously, ordered her to finish the task the party had given her, and to make sure she gave them the information they had asked for about Ula Wimmler. He could see his anger strike her across the face like a blow, making her look like the day the sheet had dropped from her breasts. Still, to quiet him, to pretend she was a good party member and a good wife (or his wife at all), she sat down at the desk and wrote.

Later, over lunch beneath the spreading tree, Dora, looking exhausted, handed him the paragraph she'd labored over for an hour:

I knew Ula Wimmler from drama school. She is a friend of Anatoli Becker, who I know through his wife, the actress Carola Becker. Ula Wimmler came from a Nazi family and was a member of the NSDAP, until she began to sympathize with us. When she stayed in Berlin last year, I gave her small things to take with her to my acquaintances in the Soviet Union. When she visited them here, she denied categorically having seen me in Berlin. This is strange, to say the least. If the party thinks it important, I could find out one thing or another.

Lusk saw that it might be a problem even to lightly link the Beckers with Ula Wimmler, but the Beckers were obviously such harmless befuddled people, he didn't see any great danger. The Soviet security services collected and evaluated all relevant evidence, and the higher councils within the party reviewed the findings; guiltless people like the Beckers needn't worry.

He handed the pages to his mother, who only glanced at them and smiled distantly, but said nothing. His father waved them away with one hand, without looking at them.

The next time Lusk visited, bearing a small stuffed bear, Marianne ran out immediately from behind her grandfather's leg. The two of them sat on the living room floor, and contentedly built workers' housing with blocks, and he read to her from children's books by his own mother, ones with a *very* nutritious content. It might, indeed, have been these sorts of stories that had led to his own commitments, and that might guide Marianne into a future like his, fighting at Lenin's direction for the equality of all the earth's people.

But would she ever enter that future, ever take up her place in the party? His daughter had lost most of her black hair, and she had dark circles beneath her eyes. Lusk wanted to enfold her in his arms and give her all the warmth from his body.

Too late for that. The doctors had said the disease had already damaged her kidneys, and maybe her heart as well. "If my beautiful granddaughter is to survive," his father said—as if the patient wasn't there—"she has to be seen by specialists who are available only in Zurich or London."

His mother pointed out the obvious, that if Lusk and Dora applied for that permission, there'd be suspicions—which, she added, "are the regrettable result of the continuing deterioration of the international situation." And besides, permission was unlikely to be granted.

His father took a spoonful of cherry jam from a ceramic jar and offered it to Marianne. His daughter was intolerably thin for a three-year-old, and her eyes didn't brighten, even when she smiled at the sweet.

That afternoon, Lusk wrote to the party to ask that his wife be allowed to take his daughter to Switzerland for ten days for a medical consultation.

There was no reply until January 8, 1938, when two agents of the NKVD came to Lusk's apartment and led him to a black sedan. Lusk went along without a struggle but not without fear. To steady himself, he repeated his plan, which would be to tell his interrogators that *a mistake had been made in the case of Ludwig (Lusk) Lask;* he would insist on his innocence and not sign anything; and soon the party would rectify this error.

2

TEN WEEKS LATER, after he signed his confession, his interrogator allowed Lusk a glass of water. After that, the guards shuffled him to a cell meant for two prisoners that he shared with six others—men whose necks had on them the first faces he'd seen since his arrest that didn't radiate a loathing for Ludwig Lask.

The cell had two bed boards that swung down from the wall, and, as the second-most-broken man (after a mathematician who looked like he'd be dead within the week), Lusk was granted one of them—"for the night," someone said, in refreshingly good German, "as tomorrow new comrades will arrive, and you won't be the baby anymore."

The next morning, Lusk met the German speaker, a thirty-year-old Russian doctor, and the other comrades, all of whom had been similarly processed, stored in a brightly lit isolation cell, until each felt in every part of his body that he'd become an object of all men's disdain, a piece of barely sentient meat that deserved to be starved and kept awake until "the membrane of consciousness and self turned so thin," the white-haired doctor said, "that our interrogators become sorcerers who can walk into our head and tell us what to do, and we still think it's our own mind that gave us the orders."

"And how much more likely is that," a former party official from Georgia said, "if a person had previously always been guided in actions by the wisdom of our Communist Party?"

"But it's not the party that tormented us," Lusk said, "not in essence," that being the position he'd come to that allowed for remnants of sanity.

The mathematician laughed, though weakly. "So you think there are two parties, Lusk? Like real and imaginary numbers?"

Not that precisely, but Lusk had concluded that the secret police had responded to the vipers biting at Soviet power by casting the widest net possible and using torture to get confessions from those mistakenly arrested; in this way, the NKVD made itself seem indispensable to a country that though surrounded was maybe less threatened internally than Yezhov pretended. Thus more police would be hired; Yezhov would increase *his* power, and soon the NKVD head would try to topple Stalin. Lusk only wished he could warn the comrade leader.

Lusk understood immediately, though, that this cell might not be the place to speak of that.

"Of what, by the way," the Georgian asked, "had Ludwig Lask been accused? At the start of his story, I mean." Lusk could tell from his tone that the man had once had authority, and from the way skin hung from his neck that he'd once been fat.

"Of making a Trotskyite joke."

"A fiver right there," the former member of the Red Army said, sounding both implacable and indifferent. Emaciated, he still had a military bearing.

"Admit to the joke and whatever else they say, comrade," the mathematician said. "Sign the first confession offered, if it's not for a capital crime. If I had," he said, "I might not be dead now."

Lusk wished he might have taken the advice that had at the beginning of his torment, not yet been offered, but instead he'd denied having made any joke (and not there or here using his brother's name). His denial, though, had been easily proved to be a lie, since a waiter had heard him, and, in a way that was efficient without being obsequious, had run to retell the jape to the security service. Alerted, the Organs had followed the traces of fecal matter left by Lusk's tarsus all the way back to his nest, the Trotskyite cell of the traitor Sten.

Lusk had said he'd never met Sten, but his interrogator had shouted that that was another lie. The late assistant director had already given the NKVD a sworn statement that Lask had conspired with him to subvert the Institute, so that it would offer the masses Trotsky's perverted interpretations of Lenin.

Lusk's consciousness might have become permeable, but there'd still been enough Lask left to scream, in perfect Russian, that that was a hideous lie, that there was nothing in the world that Lusk loved as much as the wise, prophetic, clear, and implacable voice of V. I. Lenin.

"Not even your own life, apparently," the mathematician whispered.

For weeks after, different interrogators shouted the same accusation, while the only Lusk there would ever be remained obstinate in his love for Lenin, until, finally, he'd been forbidden to use the name. For wasting the State's time, he'd been ordered to stand upright in his cell for thirty-six hours.

"Makes the legs an impacted agony," the Georgian said.

"My feet," the mathematician said, "were swollen to twice their size, and any touch was like a burning brand."

After that, guards had dragged Lusk to his next interrogation room, stripped his pants off, and a guard with a face like a hammer had beat Lusk on his legs with a thick rubber strap. They'd turned him over so Trotsky could fuck him in the ass, and they'd beat him some more, while the officer sitting behind a desk had shouted over Lusk's screams that he could stop the beating if he would lay down his arms and identify the members of the Sten cabal.

He hadn't, but that night they'd permitted him to sleep before his next interrogation, anyway, perhaps because they knew he'd wake up after a few minutes jerking about like a puppet that was having an epileptic fit. His legs had turned very surprising shades of red, blue, and yellow.

At that, three cell mates rolled up their pants to show similar, if slightly faded, bruises that meant that the suffering that Lusk had thought so intimate to him—almost his greatest achievement—was, instead, his most shared attribute. That knowledge made Lusk feel lighter but also emptier. With all their legs the same, what life belonged to Lusk Lask in particular? He turned away.

With only the mildest imitation of interest, the former soldier said, "Things got darker after that, didn't they?"

They had. His next interrogator, a man with a Tartar's face and the usual infinite hatred for him, had read him statements from the fascists Anatoli and Carola Becker in which they swore that Trotsky himself had collaborated with the Gestapo to send the implacable enemy of the people, Ludwig (Lusk) Lask, to Russia *to lead* the cell Sten had established. Lusk's orders had been to murder the new director of the institute.

"Now you're in for it," the former soldier said. "No more fiver. It's nine grams of lead to the head for that one." He seemed to take no interest or satisfaction in that development, either.

The little left of Lusk Lask, though, had been interested, had been desperate to go on living, and had told the interrogator that the Beckers had said those things because Lusk had been enraged at his wife because of a picture of her first husband in a silver frame, and she had wanted to quiet his anger.

Naturally enough, the interrogator had ignored this. Besides, he'd another document that proved the Beckers' honesty—namely, Lusk's application to get his family to safety in Switzerland before the NKVD trap closed in on him. Clearly, Lusk hated the new world Lenin and Stalin had made.

At that, Lusk had lost his mind and, without waiting for permission, had stripped off his shirt. He turned so the interrogator could see the welts the fascists had made when they'd dragged some barbed wire wrapped on a stick up and down his back in order to punish him for his love for the Party of Lenin.

The interrogator assigned to Lusk's case by that same party had laughed at the welts, which Lusk must have himself ordered the Gestapo to make, thinking they would deceive the stupid Soviets. He'd rung the brass bell on his desk to signal that the prisoner had resisted violently—he'd taken off his shirt without permission—and that guards should come to subdue him.

The former officer of the Red Army—sounding engaged with life for the first time—said, "And now comes pumping."

After which Lusk had regained consciousness in an isolation cell, his body having been laid on a bed board, and his clothes soaked in his own shit and urine.

"Not for the last time," the mathematician said.

"The stress from the pumping," the doctor added, "means the bladder never works properly again."

Day after day, guards had come to the cell, held Lusk down, and had sprayed salt on his throat over and over until it must have crusted over like a white disease. Mountains of salt were added to the gruel they allowed him, and, for nearly a week, he wasn't allowed water. To hell with Kafka, he wanted to tell Dora, it was Lusk who knew what thirst meant.

The doctor said this treatment was called *Yezhov's irony*. You lay there feeling the multitude of tiny fissures that water has made in the membranes of kidneys and bladder, and yet one's desire, stronger than any longing you had ever before experienced, was that you might have more water to drink.

"I thought," the mathematician said, "that if my betrayers at the university had turned me in for a glass of water, it was just possible I might forgive them."

At his next interrogation, the NKVD officer had been a fat man with manicured fingernails. He'd put a pile of pages on the desk next to a pen and a full glass of water.

Lusk, not trying to convince the man he wasn't a spy who should be shot, but only that he should let him have a sip of the water, had said, "Ludwig Lask's arrest was an exception to the usually accurate determinations of our great party. Ludwig Lask is, and has always been, a loyal party member."

"No," the man had said, "you're no exception. You're typical petite-bourgeoisie excrement. Look, for example, how attached you are to your name." He paused, picked up the water, and put it down again without drinking, and Lusk's eyes had followed the glass as if he were taking a neurological test. He'd wondered if he could get to the water and lap up a little before the officer rang the bell for the guards. Even the memory of that sound had made Lusk tremble like a man on a dark road whose car careens toward a wall that it never hits but never stops being about to hit.

The interrogator had looked at this quivering coward with disgust and said he couldn't possibly have ever been a loyal party member, or he would have recognized that the greatest danger to the party is not that an innocent man might be convicted but that an exception might prove the party had been wrong in its judgment, and so undermine the working class's faith in the wisdom of Stalin and Lenin.

He'd gestured for Lusk to approach the desk and read the statement the party had prepared for him.

"Which, amazingly enough," the former party official said, "didn't speak anymore of Lusk's being a German agent."

"No, it only asked me to acknowledge that I'd been a deviationist," which meant not a bullet to the head, but five years in a labor camp. That would have seemed like paradise to Lusk, if the document hadn't also listed everyone who worked at the Marxist-Leninist Institute in Moscow as coconspirators.

"On the other hand," the mathematician said, smiling weakly, "couldn't it be that your colleagues were guilty? Some of them, at least?"

"Perhaps *you* are innocent," the Georgian said, "but the institute under Sten might have been thoroughly rotten?"

"Why not lay down your arms and reconcile with the party?" the doctor said.

Alas, a small fold in Lusk's brain had stored a grain of poison: *"The reservations with which you take Evil into yourself are not yours, but those of Evil."*

"That sounds clever," the former soldier said. "What does it mean?"

It had meant that from a very momentary and completely regrettable sense of shame, and a weak but habitual desire to prove himself to be as good as a man who supposedly wouldn't lie (though who but he, himself, had ever tortured that man?), Lusk had set the papers back down next to the chipped glass of water and the bell.

The moment the pages had touched the desk, Lusk had seen that they'd reinstate the charge that he'd been a Gestapo agent, and he'd given an involuntary shriek of regret and despair.

The interrogator had looked at him as if he'd shat his britches in front of him. Still, he'd offered to give Lusk one last chance to save his wife and daughter.

"My daughter?" Lusk had said.

"My sister."
"My father."
"My son."
"My mother."

"Of course, your daughter," the interrogator had said. "Your wife is the spouse of a traitor to the Motherland. According to the legal code, she, too, is an enemy of the people. If you don't sign, I will have the bitch arrested tonight, and I will order your daughter taken to an orphanage, where the sickly little mongrel will surely die." He'd held out a pen for Lusk, and Lusk had taken the instrument into his hand.

Would it be right for him to betray fifty coworkers for a daughter he hardly knew, a girl who was a kind of fetish to him that meant Love, or the Future, when she wasn't any of those things, but only a four-year-old with damaged kidneys who wouldn't survive for very long, no matter what he did?

This calculus of years gained per person tortured was the objective materialist view, and in that perspective, which had guided Lusk's whole life, his daughter was, like all individuals, only a piece of dust, yet all that had mattered to him at that moment was that that speck should spend however much life she might have in the care of her mother, who would make sure she got enough to eat and would tuck her own blue shawl around her at night so his daughter might sleep warmly. In fact, at that moment, there was suddenly no end to the good things he'd wanted for his daughter, even that there might be penicillin for her, for this one child, even if it meant all the progress that the Socialist state had made toward industrialization would come to ruin. He'd wanted her not to die, though the great mass of humanity might die; and if life was for almost all men an endless crucifixion, he hadn't wanted it to be that for his daughter. Yes, more than anything on earth, *he'd wanted his daughter to be an exception.*

He'd signed the paper.

"You can have it now," the interrogator had said, sounding as disgusted with Lusk as before. Lusk had drained the glass, spilling some on his chin and his chest.

The mathematician died during the night, and the guards dragged the corpse away. In the afternoon, three enemies of the people were brought to the cell with bruised legs, salted throats, and similar stories to tell, and Lusk received a letter from his mother that had passed the censors the month before, when he'd still been being interrogated. Dora and Marianne, his mother wrote, had received permission to visit the doctors in Switzerland.

"That must be a lie," the Georgian said. "They don't let anyone leave."

"It's your mother trying to comfort you," the former Red Army officer said. "She's telling you that your wife is safe, when she, too, has been arrested. Later she'll write to you in the camp to tell you that your family never returned from abroad, and your wife never got in touch with her again."

"Shut up," the doctor said.

"Well, if there's any truth to your mother's letter," the former Georgian party official said, "it means that your wife has been recruited as a spy."

Yes, Lusk decided, *Dora would do that to get Marianne to a doctor.* He applauded her initiative. The party must trust that she wouldn't defect when she got to the West, must believe in her political formation, perhaps because she'd turned in others voluntarily—which made her statement betraying the Beckers a piece of good fortune, and not to be waved away with one hand, even if it had led to his own torture. But was that true if the Beckers had been shot in the Lubyanka basement? That was too complicated a moral calculus for a recently, if unexceptionally, tortured man.

Of course, even the best political formation is a frail reed. The party must think they'd another reason to believe that she wouldn't defect once she got to the West—namely, that her husband was their hostage. He laughed. Dora knew him no better than he knew her anymore. Instead, he thought, they should have threatened that they'd torture Franz Kafka.

3

AS LUSK WORKED in the mines and rivers of Kolyma, his daughter, his wife, and the ghost of Kafka became like characters in a novel Lusk barely remembered having once read. In fact, best for him to forget that book altogether, since thinking about it meant he might miss a chance to steal a bit of bread, or he might forget to properly wrap his feet so he wouldn't lose any more toes, or he might not attend to working exactly the amount needed to avoid the punishment coffin, but not so much as to die from malnutrition.

In the six months since the Lubyanka, a third of the men who'd come with him had died. Sometimes Lusk prided himself on the job he'd done carrying his life in his hands, a job that had made him suspicious, vicious, and dishonest, but in other ways had formed him into someone like the working-class comrades he'd once taught, a person able to deal with whatever happened, except that their attitude had a tincture of confidence, while his felt fatalistic. Did he still believe as they had—as he had taught them—that Marxism would show the way forward? It was hard to think about that, or about anything today. His hands had gone numb. That meant it must be near noon, though the sky was too dark to be sure.

With an effort that felt physical (and so, costly), Lusk forced himself to remember what he'd been considering, because it was important to him to once in a while think continuously about something, as if that separated one from the beasts.

And from his fellow zeks, *too?* In the absence of the party that Stalin had covered with shit (yes, he knew now that it was Stalin, not Yezhov or anyone else), Lusk was forced to try to see his own eyeball, and correct himself. Was he being petit bourgeois by trying to think, or would he die a Communist?

Well, he sometimes said, *we,* didn't he? After all, if his group didn't fulfill their work quota, he'd be among those put in the coffins and left outside to die before being dumped out into the snow. Lusk would have maimed a man from his group (except for one of the criminals) who tried to take any of his soup or bread, but if Lusk had had enough (when, though, had he ever had enough?), he could make room for a little anger that some of his fellow prisoners didn't have that much. QED: Lusk had shown that even in Kolyma the rudiments of the Communist spirit remained, one that saw the survival of the *I* and the *we* as identical.

Nearly. The man next to him had just fallen facedown in the freezing water. Snow had started; time for work would be short. No one had tried to raise the man back up, because if he lived he'd still lose some limbs and never be any use to the work group again.

That night in the barracks, the *zeks* drank cups of warm snow heated on the top of the stove. Lusk told the doctor, who'd accompanied him step-by-step from the Lubyanka, of his discovery of the Communist "we" even in Kolyma. He didn't prize the thought much anymore, but, so close to dying himself, he wanted someone to know he could still think. Though the man who knew, Lusk could see, wouldn't live much longer than he would.

In a barely audible voice, the doctor said Lusk's hypothesis seemed to be that Cucaracha's goal in the Purge had been metaphysical. He'd wanted to see if he could bring about the origin and essence of Communism again, by persecuting a group of Communists to near extinction.

Lusk, however, was wrong. First, the Boss had done it to eliminate his many opponents—present or not yet born. After that, he wanted to see to it all men feared their own will, and obeyed his, without thought. But he'd accomplished all that, the doctor whispered, and the flow of *zeks* hadn't stopped. QED: the Purge now had nothing to do with metaphysics or even politics; it was a way to provide slaves for the north.

That made sense to Lusk. First of all, it was Marxist in

its way: Stalin was an atavistic apparition of the Oriental despot. Besides, as someone had once said, in gross times, it's better to consider things in a crude way. They were all slaves who would die from hunger and cold and be replaced by other slaves. After all, unless your labor costs are nil, panning for gold was an economically inefficient way to extract the precious metal.

Yet almost as reflexively if he were saying *Ludwig Lask is innocent*, Lusk said, "Lenin would never have done this."

The doctor had met survivors of the Solovetsky Islands, but he saw how much of Lusk's scaffolding depended on a name, and he didn't argue anymore.

"The Communist spirit will never die," Lusk said, "and it will give rise to the Leninist party again." He added, in a way bound to be meaningless to anyone but the dead, "Together they form an Indestructible. The party will always renew itself."

Fortunately, by that time, the doctor had fallen into a stupor that could be confused by the uninitiated with sleep, at least for a few days; but substance was wasted by this "rest," and no cells were renewed.

The next day, a young criminal, the leader of their work group, had decided to take over the doctor's role in the debate. He had disputed the point about Lenin by hitting Lusk with his pick several times, close to his eyes. Blood poured down Lusk's face into the frigid river, and Lusk wanted to follow after. Through staggering pain and bewilderment, he remembered that he must not let himself fall into the water, or he'd be of no use to anyone anymore, and so not worth saving. He remained upright, and comrades had carried him back to the camp instead of his being left to bleed out and die.

With the warmth and the better rations of the hospital, some memories and dreams of Lusk's former life returned, which, as with frostbitten toes, was a painful process. He imagined, first, that the dark around his daughter's eyes had probably taken over her face. That misery turned him to lead.

A man learns in the camp, though, what the tragic writers (and homeopaths) already know, that you can't distract yourself from pain by dreaming of pleasure, but only by contemplating another pain, so instead of thinking of his daughter's death, he tormented himself by thinking about how if she lived, Marianne would never hear a word about Ludwig (Lusk) Lask from Dora, and if she even remembered his name, her mother would forbid her to speak it, afraid the name might lead to a prisoner in Stalin's gulag, and so to Dora's Communist past. History had turned out to be on his opponent's side. Dora Diamant would once again have become Franz Kafka's widow, and most people (not knowing the date of that obscure author's death) would probably assume that Marianne had been his child. Soon, she would probably think that, too.

As Lusk wallowed in this, the criminal who'd maimed him came to look over his work. A small, twitchy man who nonetheless spoke slowly, he explained that he'd thought only a snitch would have defended Lenin, but later he'd considered, and decided that a man who wanted to fool him wouldn't say he loved Lenin, he'd talk about hating Stalin. "Unless, that is, you were very clever."

Lusk was clever enough to know that the right answer was "I'm not very clever."

"No, I suppose not," he said, which was maybe his apology. He also told Lusk that the gray-haired old man he'd been jabbering with had been put in a punishment coffin, so he could become familiar with death before he died. His offense had been parasitism; meaning he'd become too weak to work anymore.

The thief left Lusk enough tobacco for two thin cigarettes, which must be the going price among the criminals for one eye destroyed, along with forty percent of the vision in the other.

After the hospital, it looked to Lusk as if God had dragged His greasy thumb across the world. He'd die if he returned to panning for gold, but that would mean less than nothing to those who made the work assignments. What did matter is that his mother had recently been allowed to send him food packages (no doubt her reward to him for his defense of Lenin, even though she couldn't know of it), and, without tasting even a bite, he'd given the parcels untouched (which meant after the various inspectors and clerks stole their shares) to the fat criminal who made the work assignments. The man had been generous (though he hadn't given Lusk even a crumb of food from his own parcel) and had asked if Lusk wanted to stay in the hospital as an orderly. That meant he'd have the hospital's heat, and the extra food that he could easily steal from the dying.

Lusk might not be clever, but he recognized that the name *orderly* meant *guarantee of life,* and that, in turn, meant the job was far too precious for him. Someone would eventually outbid him and take his place. Instead, he asked to be sent to the storage sheds, a job more in between life and death; it would provide some, but not complete, protection from the cold, for as long, anyway, as his mother continued to send him packages. If she died, or even forgot for a month, he'd die, too. But he didn't worry about that; he'd either deal with it or fail to deal with it when it happened.

III

1

AT AGE EIGHT, his daughter, Marianne Lask, lived in a Quaker school in Yealand, while her mother dodged fireballs in London, where she labored as a dressmaker to earn money to sustain their bodies and worked to save Yiddish culture to sustain her soul. When Marianne, just past her birthday, saw blood in the toilet bowl, she knew the red drops dissolving into the water would reach out to her mother and bring her back from the dangers in London. *It will be for your own good, Mother,* Marianne thought, those being the words her mother had used when she'd left Marianne at Yealand.

The doctor who attended at the school arranged for her transfer to the small local hospital. Marianne worried her mother might not find her there; the blood had probably told her that her daughter was at Yealand. The doctor understood that a child so often sick might both have developed some comforting fantasies and feel she needed a mother's protection; he played along and promised that if the blood didn't pass on the right route, he'd definitely help her mother get to the hospital.

For several nights in the ward, Marianne worried that the ghosts that had tormented *first father* had made the doctor forget his promise, or that they'd put up an obstacle that had made her mother give up on finding her.

Marianne knew that first father believed that there were many unseen connections between things, and one could protect oneself from ghosts by *special manipulations:* like the proper arrangement of furniture (also, when she received a letter she must make sure to open it only on a bridge). She didn't have much to work with here, though— a pad, a water glass, a picture book—but she tried different arrangements, and within a day her mother arrived.

Marianne threw her arms around her mother's neck, overcome with gratitude that she hadn't given up and, really, for everything her mother had done for her. It had to have been hard work for her to carry Marianne wrapped in blankets from the snowy Soviet Union (a place whose name, Marianne had been warned, she must never use). And when Switzerland had slammed a door as big a mountain in their faces, her mother had found a way to get them visas for England. Once in the internment camp (also a place not to be mentioned anymore) she'd found a way to get Marianne fresh vegetables so her kidneys wouldn't fail. And when they'd been released from the camp, her mother had found her a safe haven from the bombs in the Quaker school at Yealand.

This morning, her mother sat by her bed and told her and the other children in the ward stories from the Yiddish theater, a precious place because it had awakened first father to the bitterness of exile and the need for a homeland. Her mother had to keep Yiddish culture alive so that it would be there to work that same magic on the Jews who returned after the war.

Marianne, age eight, didn't understand much of this, but she loved watching her mother's round, mobile, shining face and listening to her retell the stories of the plays she'd reviewed, tales of greedy fathers who wanted their daughters to marry rich gentiles, and had to be taught a lesson that usually involved the daughter dying.

And hearing her mother's anger at the utter lack of professionalism of the performances she'd seen of these stories was especially satisfying for Marianne because, unlike the other children, Marianne understood the importance—in the way that air was important to a drowning man—of truth in art. That integrity had been what first father had lived, and you could be sure that Marianne, when she became an actress, would remember his lesson.

Her mother had stayed beside her in the ward every day, and Marianne had rested herself in the lilac smell of her powder, the salt-sweet taste of her skin, and her voice most of all, singing to her till she feel asleep. At the end of two weeks, her mother's concern had healed her; the doctors said she could return to school, and her mother to London.

"But you *could* come back to Yealand, instead," Marianne said. "They'd let you work in the kitchens again." She knew what was to come, but she had her own reasons for making her mother say it.

"Yes," Dora admitted, "I could go back to the scullery. But don't you think it's better for you if you have a happier mother? One who has such good work to do?"

"Because Yiddish is an Incorruptible?"

Her mother nodded. Marianne considered that, and had to agree, had always wanted to agree. Fairness was one of the virtues *he*'d most prized, and she had asked in the first place, so she might display that virtue, as that was something bound to please her mother.

She decided she would make a study circle (which she thought meant they would sit in a circle) at Yealand, where she and her friends would work at learning Yiddish. It would be like Quaker meeting, except that they would feel that they were in exile from somewhere wonderful. For her, of course, that would mean away from her mother.

2

SIX YEARS LATER, Marianne left Yealand Manor for Hampstead High, where she could live at home with Dora. By then her mother was busy with petition drives and fund-raising to bring a restored Hebrew and Jewish state back to life so that the Jewish people would finally have their place of renewal and safety.

Never had these things been more needed. Eight of Dora's siblings—Marianne's unknown (though permissible to speak of) aunts and uncles from her mother's side, and all of Kafka's sisters, had been murdered by the Nazis. Very few souls would return who could make use of the culture her mother had protected during the war, so that it might awaken in them the bitterness of exile, which the Jews of Europe had anyway otherwise learned. They needed now to learn the modern Hebrew her mother and Kafka had studied together in their room in Berlin, and make themselves ready for their Return.

They both believed Marianne was to be an actress (for her mother said she had a wonderfully elegant look, expressive eyes, and a voice of both surpassing gentleness and great directness), and it might well be at the theater Kafka's friend, Max Brod, managed in Tel Aviv. Toward that end, Marianne began to learn Hebrew herself. As with Yiddish (or English, or German), she turned out to be a very good student.

Just after Israel's rebirth, another miracle: Marianne Steiner, a niece of Franz Kafka's, had found them, and niece and widow had wept with wonder and joy, each at the other's survival. The younger Marianne was at first suspicious of this thin, attractive woman, with her stiff bearing, who, as a Kafka, might feel she had the right to judge Marianne. But she turned out to be more than kind, and offered Dora money from the royalties for Kafka's books, the ones that, ineffectively destroyed by her mother, were now almost everywhere. At first, her mother refused—the books were an Indestructible, and so belonged, like Yiddish or the Jewish State, to everyone and no one, but when Marianne—*her* Marianne—required treatment at Pembury Hospital, Dora had no choice but to accept it.

Besides, with these extra funds, she said, she might also manage to save enough money for a visit to Israel, and at least see the country to which she'd planned to immigrate before she had met Kafka. The two of them had also talked of going together, but they both knew, given his lungs, that was a fantasy. "We would talk about opening a restaurant together," her mother said, "with Franz as the waiter." That compounded fantasy by fantasy, Marianne Steiner said. Her uncle, she said, would no doubt have carried the food very carefully, yet it would always have remained only a dream for the would-be diners.

A trip to Israel, Marianne knew, was impossible now, and her mother said it only to make her daughter feel that it would be all right to take charity for Marianne's care by pretending in this way that it was also for her.

But then it turned out (such were the myriad connections between events), the famous Mr. Brod had arranged for the city of Tel Aviv to sponsor a trip for her mother to give talks about Kafka (and perhaps to leave something precious in the homeland, as her mother, of course, knew that special objects could move the spiritual powers). Soon after, Marianne had another attack. Not very serious, the doctors said, she'd probably need to stay in the ward for only a month, but Marianne had become afraid of Pembury Hospital, as if it were an inbetween place whose inhabitants were neither alive or dead and might remain that way forever.

She understood, though, why her mother needed to go to Israel to know that the Jewish people would survive—and perhaps to see the life that might have been if she hadn't met Kafka. "If it hadn't been for him," she told her mother when she visited, "you'd have been spared so much." She had her own agenda in saying that.

"But look at all I would have lost if I hadn't met Franz," her mother said. "And most of all, if I'd gone to Palestine, I wouldn't have had you."

Those words had been Marianne's goal, but now that she heard them they only made the world spin around her dizzyingly. Her mother had told a Yiddish playwright with very large ears that a child of Kafka's would have been a gift to the world. Marianne wanted to ask, *Do you think I'm a gift, too?*

As if she knew the question, her mother said, "You're my life's greatest joy, Marianne. I'll miss you terribly, and will write every day, so that it will be as if you were with me."

3

TWO YEARS LATER, when Marianne had returned to the hospital for an operation that might both save her life and let her have a more normal one, her mother's kidneys began to fail. Within the vast cascading and compounding terror, her mother's arrival also felt like a reprieve. The hospital was even kind enough to let them have beds next to each other; and this stay in the inbetween became almost as good as the best time in her life, when she and her mother had been on the train that took them across Europe, and they'd been forbidden to leave the car when the train stopped along the way. Her mother, as anyone could see (and everyone did), had a special inner light (one that either had attracted or been provided by first father). She was a warm, enthusiastic, compassionate being, someone to whom people were naturally drawn, any one of whom might distract her from her daughter. On the train, those people couldn't find her; and the ones already there might ask too many questions, and were to be avoided. In fever dreams, sometimes, if Marianne was fortunate, she even returned there.

The hospital wasn't as effective a barrier to others as the train. During visiting hours, her mother had the company of friends from the Yiddish theater, from the school, and from *his* world, too, scholars of his work, none of whom talked much to Marianne, though they often talked about her.

Her mother made her visitors promise to take care of her little girl, and Isaac Chazzan, the same Yiddish playwright who'd heard what a gift Kafka's child might have been, turned to her to make the vow, though it was clear to Marianne that this man, who was only ten years older than her mother, was so frail that even if her own operation failed, she would out-live him.

He also must have read Marianne's mind. He said, "Don't worry, child. I plan to be around a long time. Long past the time anyone has a use for me." He smiled with blackened teeth, though it horrified him to think the world might be so arranged that he'd live longer than this odd, bright-eyed girl.

Soon after that promise, Dora began to say nonsensical things about the Tel Aviv restaurant she worked in where Franz was a waiter.

Dora's hands began to paw the thin blanket, looking for his silver brush so she could take care of his hair.

"It's not here, Mama. You left it at a kibbutz in Israel."

"If you're a Jewish girl," her mother said, "you must go to Israel."

Marianne wept, for her mother, and because her mother no longer knew who she was.

"Israel will heal and protect you."

No, Marianne thought, the only thing that could protect her would be her mother's watching over her, in this life or from the next.

A day later, her mother entered a more profound *inbetween*, one from which her words couldn't be heard anymore, and Marianne sat by her bedside all day, confronting the emptiness now and the emptiness to come. Years ago, a nurse had told her that coma patients could hear those around them, even though they couldn't reply. Marianne had said to the nurse, "Then God must be a coma patient." Was that an aphorism worthy of *him*? No, Marianne had nothing to give her mother—no hairbrush, no aphorisms, nothing that could pull her back to life, to her.

Powerless and bereft, terrified and angry, Marianne stroked her mother's stiff gray hair and told her she loved her, told her that over and over, until her mother stopped breathing, and then, in case death might be like a coma, she went on telling her mother her love for her even after.

4

MARIANNE, AGE EIGHTEEN, had spent so much time inbetween that she'd never been to a restaurant or the post office or made love to a man. Her kidneys had improved now, and she was looking forward to all those things. The world made her anxious, of course, but it also seemed like a colorful and exciting place, filled not only with dangers but with possible pleasures.

On the other hand, since her mother's death, buses terrified her. Fortunately, she found a job within walking distance of her new flat, where, wonderfully enough, she'd be a secretary in an insurance company, as he'd been. She had the odd idea that as imitation was flattery, this might please him (so to speak) in that comfortable realm great spiritual beings must be given in which to live out the afterlife. If she pleased him, she would surely please her mother, and she would continue to feel her mother's sustaining presence.

One or two old friends from the Yealand School, the old Yiddish playwright, and Kafka's niece also came to visit her. Marianne Steiner even helped her apply for British citizenship, which would entitle her to free health care, which she needed now not because of her kidneys but because she had sharp electrical pains in the nerves of her legs, as if malign spirits wrote on them with high-voltage prods.

After several terrifying bus trips needed to get to the office where one filed the application for citizenship, and a long wait in a queue, they got to the necessary wicket, where the indifferent official had to watch her sign the document.

Marianne hesitated. To get citizenship she had to declare that Ludwig (Lusk) Lask was dead, and she didn't know if that was true. She wondered if Kafka would have lied to get health care, to get love, to get more life. Doing something of which first father might disapprove might make her mother withdraw from her.

She stared at the pen in her hand. The noise from the people in the government office line grew louder and louder. If she signed, she felt she might (such are the hidden connections in the world) even kill Ludwig Lask, as if he, too, were maybe in between life and death, and her signature would decide things once and for all.

"If you don't sign, how will you pay for the hospitals if you need them?" Marianne Steiner said.

That sounded almost like a prediction; and so Marianne Lask traded her father's life for British citizenship.

5

OR SO SHE'D THOUGHT. Two years after that, a policeman came to her door at the behest of the mayor of London. He had a message from the German Democratic Republic and Ludwig (Lusk) Lask, the man she'd supposedly destroyed with her pen stroke. Marianne Lask began to shiver uncontrollably, from anxiety, but also from expectation. She would have an earthly father, and that, she felt, might be the way to the world she still found it so hard to enter.

At that, she couldn't talk, or stop shaking, and the policeman, thinking she'd had an epileptic fit, went to call for an ambulance. Marianna Lask didn't need it, but if she had, she was fortunately, as a British citizen, part of the National Health Service.

IV

1

AND AS A CITIZEN, she could also get the passport she needed to visit her father. A year after that policeman's visit, Marianne and Ludwig (Lusk) Lask were on their way back from a performance by the Berliner Ensemble. They walked past mounds of uncleared rubble, craters filled with water that looked like septic lakes, façades of buildings that seemed portentous stage sets. These ruins embarrassed Lusk in front of his daughter. How could the party be so slow in having the remains of the disaster carted away, be so behindhand in rebuilding? Or did they leave the stones there intentionally, a Stalinist sort of propaganda: *See what happens if you take the capitalist path—it leads to your destruction.* How could he ever ask his daughter to believe in *this* party? But, of course, he didn't want that; he wanted her to know what the party had been under Lenin, and what it could become again—the imperishable force of brotherhood to which he'd once devoted his life.

They started to cross the avenue, and a Soviet lorry, knowing it could afford to be indifferent, even vicious, to everything German, nearly ran his daughter down. He dragged her back.

"Thank you," his daughter said, very quietly.

Lusk thought his daughter seemed at once terrified and oddly pleased by it all, not simply at being alive, but that *he* had been her salvation. He smiled fondly at her, both the fondness and the smile being so unexpected that he couldn't walk for a moment. He looked at her.

His daughter was certainly pretty, in the way of a forest sprite; she had short brown hair, a fine thin frame (not buxom like her mother), and long legs, like his. Her bright, sharp eyes might also be like his—as they'd once been. Should he tell her how pretty she seemed—was that the sort of thing permitted to fathers who hadn't seen their children for seventeen years and were almost strangers? Should he put his arm around her? Was that allowed to someone in his peculiar position? Instead, he said, "Is your coat warm enough?"

She nodded yes, and they started forward again, past a group of Soviet soldiers who were smoking and laughing. The CPSU treated the German party not like a younger brother but as a vassal in need of brutal supervision day to day. Lusk tasted the salt of truth in the Soviet attitude. The troops couldn't leave until the DDR was cleansed of Nazism and no longer threated by the West, but he believed, too, that they would never leave. He suspected that the DDR was only another labor camp constructed to benefit the socialist Motherland.

·   ·   ·

The Soviet soldiers reminded Marianne of her father's past, and she asked why he had been arrested. As soon as she'd said it, though, she wondered if that was a question allowed to someone in her position.

He could reply, *Ludwig Lask was an exception, arrested by mistake.* Of course, that meant he'd wintered in a gulag stuffed with exceptions. And it meant the admission of something worse than the Soviet party's brutality and incompetence; it meant that at the time of his arrest he had been innocent; he truly hadn't been part of the delegate leader's opposition. As that recent corpse Brecht had aptly said, "The more innocent the arrested are, the more they deserve to be shot." Lusk's guiltlessness was his shame, even if it hardly compared with the guilt of the famous coward who, even in exile, had never said one public word against Stalin, or come to visit his old friend Bertha Lask, either. Too busy? More likely fear—the Stasi and the Soviets would be curious why he consorted with a woman whose two sons had once been declared enemies of the people.

"I don't know why I was arrested." That was true, anyway. For slave labor, probably, but he wasn't going to say that to his daughter. That name, the true one, he knew, would reveal him as utterly pathetic.

They neared the cement housing block where Lusk and his mother lived. It, too, spoke of Stalin's legacy, as if communal life should also always mean denial, pain, difficulty.

Marianne remembered her grandmother saying, "I wish you could have seen our house before the war. It was a great gathering place. Even Brecht used to visit." Marianne thought of the play they'd just seen, the woman dragging her cart from battle to battle in Europe, her children spilling from it to their deaths. "That mother in the play," she said, "she reminded me of yours."

"Your grandmother?" Lusk said, meaning to assert a lineage that would include him. Besides, that title had brightened his mother's eyes, which otherwise often looked like they, too, had been hit by a pick. "No, she didn't think she'd profit from a war." He began to tell her about her famous pacifist play, her coming to Communism because its struggle, however violent, would eventually end war.

"You're proud of her."

"I am." To prove her grandmother's excellence, he described all that his mother had done to free him, told his daughter about the sad train of begging letters to Ulbricht, one of the leaders of the GDR. And when Lusk, by purest chance, had seen an article about a friend of Kafka's (and *not the wife of Ludwig Lask*) who'd died, and it had mentioned her surviving daughter, it was her grandmother who'd gotten permission from Ulbricht for Lusk to communicate with England, and her friends had also helped get the visas for Marianne's visit. "I suppose those things are like the best of the mother in the play."

"My grandmother knows Ulbricht," Marianne replied, but Lusk couldn't tell from her tone if she was impressed or offering an argument that she was like the woman in Brecht's play.

2

THE ACQUAINTANCE of Ulbricht's had waited up for them. Marianne embraced the gray-haired old lady and kissed her cheek over and over, as if it might disappear at any moment.

In the little kitchen, Lusk got the kettle on, and Bertha told Marianne what Dora had once said about Kafka and the tea. Memories of Dora, after all, were what linked them.

"I remember that story," Marianne said. "The carefully brewed tea that never arrives."

Lusk measured out the leaves, and for many reasons (to show his love, because his vision was partial, because tea was expensive), he did it carefully. "I suppose," Lusk said, "you could think of him as keeping the idea of things made with real concern alive, and at the same time showing that it couldn't be done under capitalism." He poured the water in. "But it's ridiculous to think the workers need that further proof, no?"

Marianne said, "Communism will be a world where one can be both caring *and* have some hot tea." She felt smarter around her father. He had made her think she might take a course in nursing when she returned to London.

"Lovely, you two," her grandmother said. "May I use this in a book?"

Lusk made a sour face. He didn't want in any way to be linked with Kafka's name—not even as a critic. He brought the teapot to the small wood table.

"My mother said that when they lived in Berlin, during the inflation, he would make his way to the central part of town, so he could queue with the others for tea, even though he didn't want to buy any."

"Where blood flowed, his must flow, too," Lusk said, both mocking and sad.

Marianne squeezed her father's hand. It pleased her that he knew the story, as if it gave them a family life, though lived in different stages and places. She hoped that having a family would be a protection against what the ghosts were doing to her, like the shooting pains in her legs that felt like writing.

"It's ridiculous to go to look for suffering," Lusk said. "If Kafka had led a more active life, suffering would have found him." Or he could have just stayed home, and it would have conveniently come for him in a big black car. Anyway, Lusk had heard enough about Kafka for a night.

Perhaps Bertha was sick of him, too—or simply tired. She left father and daughter to get to know each other better. Maybe, too, she didn't want to be there if the talk turned again to Lusk's own suffering.

And as soon as she left, Marianne asked what had happened to his left eye. But the moment she asked, she regretted the question. He said nothing, only stared at her unseeingly through his thick glasses. One eye was dead, but the other eye required the strongest lens to see at all. A right lens had wastefully been made to match the other, though it could do nothing except make the blind eye look like a monstrous wound—or, because it was paired with its living brother, like a corpse.

The memory of the blow that had destroyed his eye, and the river that would have killed him, made his body tremble from the chill. He drove the nails of his hands into his palms until he could speak again. "A thief hit me because he thought I was a snitch." He prayed she hadn't seen him shake.

Marianne heard the drop in temperature in his toneless voice, and it gave her a bad chill as well. Her father seemed almost indifferent with others, but never with her. That preference for her was something she hadn't always felt with her mother, who didn't act indifferently to anyone, but had a warm concern for all. Her father's choosing her, in particular, was a gift of great value, but now it seemed to have been withdrawn.

Still, if she was ever to have a father, her father had to have a past. She had no choice but to ask once more: "Were you a snitch?"

"No." He admired her implacability, found her persistence both painful and touching. But he had to be careful. He didn't want Marianne to know that the cause of the Purge had been to make him and others into slaves, and he didn't want her ever to see him tremble again.

3

FOR THE NEXT FEW DAYS, Lusk and his daughter walked about the winter city, or sat drinking weak coffee in a café that made no concessions to bourgeois—or proletarian—decoration. Like an interrogator, Marianne returned (and returned him) to Kolyma repeatedly. And such was a daughter's power that since she asked about the camps, he tried to answer. Odd, how rare these questions had been from anyone since his return. Maybe unlike the others, she hadn't heard a thousand similar stories, or didn't feel his stories were in competition with their own suffering during the war. Or that they were an accusation. Marianne wasn't complicit, as every Communist, including the victim, Ludwig (Lusk) Lask, felt himself to be.

He described being tied to a sleigh and dragged to the mine for being last out of the barrack his first year, or told how he and another man had to pull a cart like oxen, with leather thongs on their foreheads and chests, and she simply nodded with a birdlike motion, as if checking something from a list. Impossible, yet he would have said that his stories somehow comforted her.

And, indeed, they had. Marianne felt her father's stories made the horrible things come out of hiding, and showed that if one had sufficient strength, *the way her father did*, they could be survived. Her father's legs had been damaged, his eyes nearly blinded, but he could still deal with whatever was thrown at him.

A policeman, for example, who asked, in a most unkindly way, for them to show their papers. They'd been seen, he said, walking about. Where was their camera?

They had no camera, her father said, in a voice Marianne thought neither polite nor aggrieved. And he had his papers in his overcoat, and a whole sheaf of hers, prepared for just this eventuality.

The policeman left. Her earthly father had already saved her from lorries and from being arrested as a spy. She imagined standing on tiptoe and kissing him on the cheek, a thing she suspected daughters might do. The father who cared about her opinion would be pleased, she thought, but the cold person from Kolyma might be indifferent, and that would be painful for her. Best, she decided, not to try.

She put her arm around him, though. Had there been even five men, she wondered, with whom she'd done this? His absence had been the problem; this was where a girl was meant to practice. Her time with her mother had been lived mostly in hospitals; now her kidneys had grown stronger and her soul would surely follow. Her father's presence would both protect her from any malicious unseen things and calm her anxieties without her having to take the pills the doctors said might make her tremble. She was sure a new epoch would begin for her.

4

MARIANNE HAD TO RETURN to London, and Lusk, lacking party membership still, was repeatedly denied the right to visit her, or to send her money, supposing he should ever put aside any from his minor position at the Marxist-Leninist Institute, reediting already reedited texts. "It will be years before she can save enough for a ticket to Berlin," Lusk told Natalie Kolman, another survivor of Stalin's camps, and his one friend at the institute, or in the world, though Lusk did think that *a friend* might have said, *Of course she'll visit you again,* so perhaps the very basis of their friendship was that each tolerated in the other the way they fell short as friends.

As for his daughter, all he would have of her companionship for a long while would be her letters—about her nursing course ("the other students had seemed a sad and harmless lot to me; but then, as it turns out, it was like Kafka said to Mother once, they, like me and most other animals, also have teeth"), about her difficulty with buses to get to that course ("when I get on I feel like I'm entering the belly of a monster, like Jonah, but with no God to make sure he'll spit me back up at my destination, only a very human conductor"), about her nervous and cruel boss at the office where she worked ("her hands flutter in the air and in my stomach at the same time"), or about Dora's friends, like Kafka's niece, apparently also a Marianne, who took her to the beach, or had her to her house for holidays ("where I am tolerated as the remembrance of my mother, and as repository of her memories of another").

Lusk's own daily life was conducted through a fogged glass, and if Natalie Kolman's silence was company, it wasn't companionship that brought any other color or form to him; only these letters from his daughter let Lusk glimpse the variegated world again. How, he wondered, could the name *daughter* be so powerful? But he remembered that once the entire Marxist-Leninist Institute in Moscow had discovered the power that word had over him when he had condemned them to the Lubyanka.

He wrote Marianne that anyone who'd experienced her company valued her for herself. Or he told her about his day's lunch, or what he'd read at the institute. Or . . . but he soon ran out of events to write about, or any interest in writing them. What he wanted to do, again and again, was to give her a better answer to the question *Why were you arrested?* and not just him but so many others. The *many* was the crux of the *again;* the enormity of the gulag over-flowed any explanation that he could provide for it; he was like someone, who—without any recourse to parable— was trying to explain not why a person died but why there was death in the world at all. Why had the flowers of Lenin's party pledged their obedience to the Gardener of Human Happiness, who had then immediately ripped so many of them up by the roots? He needed to explain those things, but in a way that let her see the enduring value of the Communist spirit—equality for all people— and that the need of the people for the guidance of a Lenin-ist party to realize that spirit, remained.

"You shouldn't write about any of that to her," his mother said when he told her about his letters. "They just upset you, and when the Stasi reads them, it could delay your reinstatement." She paused, scared of her own words and of their possible effect on Lusk. "Or it could lead to an arrest."

5

MARIANNE'S MOTHER had withdrawn to a middle distance, but her father's presence (given to her simply for being his daughter) had compensated. The intense pain in her legs, which felt like someone's malicious graffiti, had continued, but she could talk less anxiously to people in her new office, even the men. And thanks to her father's protection, she could—if she found a seat by the aisle in front—take buses.

It helped to take her father's letters on the tram with her to read on her way to the nursing course. She barely ever attended to the first part of his letters, though, the kind and unconvincing words about her, the news of difficulties getting doctor's appointments for her grandmother (she was having fainting spells), or about the bland sausage with too much cereal that he apparently ate absolutely every day for lunch, all things that she thought of as written by *inbetween* father, who remembered from when he'd been fully alive that friendship meant he should share fragments of his life, even ones about which he felt indifferent. But her real, her *living*, father always stopped that nonsense and wrote to her what he cared most about: that she not draw the wrong moral from the story told by his maimed body and lose hope for the Communist enterprise.

Marianne knew he wanted to convince her of all this not because of her great intellect but because he didn't want his daughter to think her father's life had been wasted. She'd never been important in that way before—it was someone else's opinion her mother valued most—and she usually found it immensely nourishing to be needed by her parent, especially as he was (at the same time) himself a man of such great inner strength.

Today, though, she found this need also unsettled her, though despite her growing anxiety, she had to continue the trip or she'd miss her first exams. The bus bumped along, and the repetitive letter (*Did the party have a choice but to industrialize with brutal rapidity in order to defend the Bolshevik Revolution? . . . And in the absence of long education of the worker by the market, what was left but the lash and prison?*) began to seem as anxious as her own chest felt. Worse, it was littered with question marks, as if he wasn't asking her to agree with his thoughts but wanting her to tell him what to think.

She saw that the bus would crash at the next roundabout, and knowing that a vision was probably absurd was never any help. Thank God the driver had to stop. She pushed past the lady with the bags and managed to make it off, but she was miles from the school, and miles from home. Safest, though, to turn back.

And not to go the next day, either. By the third day, she

felt like it wasn't worth the pain the trip would bring her. She would never catch up with the rest of the pack.

6

THE EMPTY WEEKS between Marianne's letters began to increase like the grain in DDR sausage, and the brief accounts of her day at the office (no mention of nursing anymore) became as flat and smudged as Lusk's own barely binocular world.

"Do you think I offended her?" he asked Natalie. They lay in bed, having made love (in between his trips to the toilet) as reluctantly as they talked. Natalie, closer to his own height than Dora, was meager in body and gesture, where his former wife, as he remembered her, had been generous. On the other hand, Natalie never spoke of her first husband other than to say, *Shot in the Lubyanka basement.*

"Your letters," she said, "sound like a man going over and over an unhappy love affair." She gave a small turn to her lips. Natalie, child of the proletariat, thought capitalism degraded and Communism enslaved. She had a most corrosive smile. "Maybe your daughter feels jealous of Lenin."

As he once had been of Franz Kafka. He told Natalie his worry that his daughter now too much imitated that sad, misguided, and misguiding man.

"She wants to be a writer?"

"Not that, fortunately. But that image of the bus as a beast, that sounds like something Kafka might have written. My daughter's been taught that there are two communicating worlds, this one and an utterly nonexistent one."

"Not all people are materialists."

"Not all are filled with fear, either. And she's made herself as painfully sensitive as he was, too." Kafka, he thought, would have died during his first day of interrogation. The interrogator's contempt would have turned him into a cockroach. "And I think she's even more chaste than Kafka was."

"Fathers," Natalie said, "are often wrong about that." She lit a cigarette.

"Maybe so, but he had so much self-hatred, he's the wrong model for her, or for anyone."

"Better she worshipped her father, you think? And Lenin, of course."

Better, he thought, that she followed nothing but her own heart, but that wasn't something he could say to Natalie. She undoubtedly would have used a *zek*'s worst opprobrium, and said that he'd been sentimental.

That week, Bertha Lask (the acquaintance of Ulbricht's), received a gift from the party, a book bound in red leather with gold letters stamped on the cover, *Speech to the Twentieth Party Congress*. Lusk began reading standing up in the hall, but by the end he had slumped against the wall, astounded by what he'd read—each of Stalin's crimes enumerated and repeated to "applause and consternation in the hall"—but more astounded that the speech did nothing to warm or renew him. Instead, he felt an even more cavernous emptiness in his chest, as if the delegate leader's words had turned his body into a shell, a papier-mâché doll. A small child could easily have stuck a hole in him and wiggled a finger where his heart had once been.

"You expect too much," his mother said that evening. "He admits everything, Lusk, but the truth can't give us our lives back." She put a piece of herring and some black bread on the table for his dinner. "Or your brother's life." Her worn face, Lusk thought, had lines for each year her children had spent in Stalin's prison. "But look, he's rededicated our party to the principles of Lenin." She poured Lusk a cup of tea—brewed with at least a modicum of concern, he could be sure—and put it by his hand.

Lusk hadn't expected his life back, but he felt as though his emptiness and his questions could only line his mother's face more, as if she would feel that really he was saying, *Why did you lead your sons to slaughter?* He stared at the herring, but cardboard figures have no appetite. He couldn't imagine picking up his fork and eating.

"Khrushchev will purge the party," she said. "He will give the workers their guide again. You'll see, you'll be reinstated soon."

Lusk sipped the weak tea. Most probably his mother was right on all fronts; light was being shone into every corner, yet Lusk remained blinded by the darkness of the camps.

China had awakened, he reminded himself. The Korean party had fought the Americans to a draw. The Vietminh had overrun the French. Even if he remained hollow, he could write to his daughter of these signs that Lusk's life, Lusk's cause, hadn't been in vain.

That conclusion let him pick at the fish.

7

MARIANNE RECEIVED A LETTER from her father with the good news about Khrushchev's speech. As he'd promised her, the spirit of Lenin had proved itself an Indestructible. Letters from him about Mao and Ho Chi Minh that sounded still more fulfilled had followed, and when Marianne Steiner—tall, self-possessed, and with hair stylishly cut short in an intriguing geometric pattern—came to visit Marianne Lask, Ludwig Lask's daughter felt both proud and anxious that she could meet *his* gracious niece with an inheritance all her own, a *restored* and powerful father who didn't ask but told her what he and the party thought about history—told *her,* in particular.

Still, as if bound by an archaic injunction, Marianne didn't tell the Other Marianne about the change in Lusk Lask, whose name or letters she rarely mentioned. Instead, she served her some tea and a plate of biscuits, and asked politely if she could borrow money from the estate, "for travel."

"Wonderful," Marianne Steiner said. She'd long worried, she said, that Marianne's life had become only bed-sit and office, office and bed-sit, and (though she didn't say as much) she felt deeply for this girl, this fellow sufferer. "Where will you go?"

"I don't know. Someplace warm, I think."

Marianne didn't see through the lie, and immediately arranged for money to be transferred to Marianne's account.

8

FATHER AND DAUGHTER spent most of her time in Berlin sitting by Bertha Lask's bedside, in a barely heated, very crowded hospital ward that was only marginally better furnished than the one at Kolyma. Lusk's mother had had the brain hemorrhage that all the doctors had known her dizziness predicted, though none of them, it seemed, could do anything to prevent it.

It left her face looking slack, white, almost dead. "She's in some in-between place," Lusk said pointlessly.

Marianne took her father's mangled hand so his strength might flow into her. "How did you know that's what I called the hospitals?"

"I didn't."

"The inbetween. I guess I mean in between home and the grave. I had the silly fantasy that my mother might forget me there, and I'd be changed by the *inbetween,* and even if I got out of the hospital, the living wouldn't be able to hear me."

"Your mother would never forget you," Lusk said, and he felt how his defense of Dora made him a good father.

"She didn't forget, of course. But I was so afraid of her leaving me there that I always tried to be a perfect child, one who never disobeyed and didn't complain about anything." She omitted, though, that she also tried to do the sorts of things *first father* liked, even the kabbalistic manipulation of objects, because her mother had especially loved all his ways. "Of course, I also did complain about her leaving me, even though I knew that was the most annoying thing I could complain about, and it might cause her to leave me. I couldn't stop myself."

She couldn't stop herself today, either. Lusk could hear the choked, insistent tone of a heart-divided young person who feared she might not be believed when she accused her parent of an injustice. So Lusk *must* hear about her mother and her, and right now, even as his own mother lay dying. In another way, though, her selfishness was reassuring; it was how children acted, playing one parent against the other.

"But she never left you," Lusk said, hoping to approve of himself again, "did she?"

"She did, sometimes," Marianne said. Marianne thought her honesty would strengthen the bond between them, and so his protection of her. "When I was at Yealand, she went to London to work for Yiddish. And she went to Israel while I was in the hospital. She had to save the Indestructibles. I never understood why something no one could destroy needed so much effort just to keep alive."

Lusk offered his daughter some chocolate to comfort her, a great luxury in the Workers' State. Since Khrushchev's speech he'd spent far too much money on it, by way of celebration of the party's reform, or compensation for all that it still hadn't accomplished in his hollow chest.

"Mother said she had to go to Israel to heal her soul."

"Did it work?"

"Maybe. But it turns out the soul and the body aren't joined the way *he'd* thought. She got sick, anyway." She felt dizzy when she said that, like a tightrope walker looking down.

Lusk saw an opportunity to wean her from Kafka's pernicious influence. "He wasn't a god, the way your mother thought," Lusk said, and he heard the choked tone in his own voice now, himself thrown back to the unfairness of his marriage. "He was only ever a bewildered man, just like the rest of us. *More* terrified and bewildered than the rest of us, maybe."

"*I* never thought he was a god," she said. "A broken sort of angel, maybe, crippled when he fell. Some such thing, anyway."

"Good," he said. "I'm glad you don't worship him."

"I don't." Her mother had, though.

But he didn't believe her. Some greater exorcism was necessary for a habit so rooted, though as with Dora, he couldn't imagine what it would be.

He got up and stood looking down at his mother's still face, as if she might have the answer.

"You should tell her you love her," Marianne said.

Talking to someone who couldn't hear sounded like more Kafka nonsense. "I love her, Marianne, but I can't do that," he said. "It would be like talking to a ghost, and,

137

unlike Kafka, I'm not foolish enough to believe in ghosts." He sat down, put his arm around his daughter.

A nurse came by a few minutes later and leaned over the immense form. She stood up with some extra solemnity to her bearing and drew the corpse's eyelids down with a single finger. Lusk was glad his daughter was with him. It meant he wouldn't let his mind go toward the wall.

That protection would be lost soon; Marianne would have to return to London immediately after the cremation, and without party membership, Lusk would never be allowed to visit her. His greatest sadness, for now, anyway, wasn't for his mother's death, but that he might never see his daughter again.

A month later, Ludwig (Lusk) Lask, as his mother had promised, was rehabilitated, and his membership in the Communist Party was reinstated, first by the Soviet party and then by its fraternal brother in the German Democratic Republic. He read the letter in the same dark entryway where he'd read Khrushchev's speech, and felt not joy for himself, or confidence in the party's renewal, but a greater loneliness: the person who'd have been most pleased by this, the one who understood the meaning for which his life had once been lived, was no more.

Fortunately, the reinstatement also meant that he could at least apply for permission to travel to England, where he could tell his living daughter of his love for her.

9

A YEAR LATER, Ludwig Lask waited in Marianne's small flat in London for her friends to arrive for the unveiling of the hidden father. His daughter was neatly, if a little nunishly, dressed in a white shirt and a well-tailored brown skirt and jacket. Thirty-seven years old, she looked and acted much younger than her years. She was, Lusk feared, too much untouched by life outside these three rooms.

She arranged and rearranged biscuits on a plate. Some had chocolate on them, and it was all Lusk could do not to stuff them in his pockets. He felt as if something momentous would happen here—as if her friends could decide if he was suitable to become her father again—a feeling that reminded him of the interviews before receiving his party membership, which had also occurred in small, drab rooms, though without biscuits. To calm himself, he sat on the sofa, crossed his palms on his lap, and looked toward the heater. Was it coin-operated? he wondered.

Marianne thought his glance had been toward the molding, and that he'd seen that she'd hidden the silver picture in a drawer. But before she could try to find out, the guests had started to arrive.

Four, in total. Was this a nucleus, Lusk wondered, or his daughter's whole universe? There was a girl with prominent teeth from her office; the still attractive middle-aged niece of Kafka's who shared his daughter's first name, and her beefy husband, who worked at the BBC. The two of them had spent the war here, had returned to Czechoslovakia, and then come back again as refugees, the man said in a deep voice and with ominous irony, "from Victorious February," the triumph of the party in Czechoslovakia. The last guest was an older man, Isaac something, who'd been in the Yiddish theater with his former wife. He had a familiar face; but the tribe of which he and Lusk were a part looked, Lusk believed, more and more similar as they aged.

There was room at Marianne's table for only three of them, and the guest of honor—or was he the accused? Marianne Steiner sat with the stiff back of a former Soviet officer and the disdainful look of an interrogator, as if, as a Kafka, she had the right to judge everyone. Steiner's husband stood behind her chair with a hawk's nose and a face as impassive as a guard who would pump water into the stomach of the honored guest as soon as his wife rang the bronze bell on her desk.

Lusk was too much reminded of his past, and he stumbled in his English today. In Berlin, the War and the Wall cast a shadow on everyone, and helped hide his difficulties; here, he feared his daughter would see how much outside life Lusk remained.

Marianne hovered near her father. She thought fatigue had made him quiet. Grieving for his mother, along with the heavy responsibility of party membership, had turned his hair gray and made him labor for breath when they walked through museums. But he was still, she could tell, spiritually strong. She put her hand on his shoulder for a moment to feel that strength and then went to the kitchen to get more biscuits.

Lusk was delighted by the touch. He ate another biscuit, and made an effort to fit in. "It's hard for you, no?" he said to the playwright. "Writing in a dying language?" Stupid thing to say, Lusk knew, both mean and a cliché. What he really wanted to say was, *It's not an Indestructible.*

The old playwright stared at him. Lusk couldn't bear the magnified blurred eyes that were so much like his own, and turned his attention to the man's ears, which would someday be his, too, and which were like the shells of huge mollusks that had little beards peeking from the holes where the animal hid.

"Dying, yes," the man said, "but not dead." He smiled with blackened teeth. "It's always been the language of an in-between place."

Lusk saw Marianne start with fear at the coincidence of words, Dora having taught their daughter the Kafka gospel that all things were linked, so a bird or an old Yiddish writer might speak your secrets. He felt a gust of fury toward Kafka's malign spirit for the way it had trapped his daughter, made her as neurotically superstitious as a tribesman or a Hasidim.

"And the population of the inbetween grows by the day, doesn't it?" the old man said. "You're one of us, too, aren't you?"

Lusk couldn't help himself; he nodded.

"Don't worry, Lusk. We Jews have learned that between dying and dead can take a very long time."

"Have you pronounced a blessing on me," Lusk said, "or a curse?"

The man raised his huge eyebrows and nodded in sad, if ironic, agreement to Lusk's irony.

"The whole Soviet block," Marianne Steiner said. "Isn't it all another in-between place?" She stared at Lusk, as if he'd driven her out of Prague. "People not quite alive, mouthing nearly dead slogans."

That, too, was a cliché. But his daughter looked scared for him. He had to show her that a man who could survive interrogation in the Lubyanka could make short work of Kafka's niece, and all that Kafka might represent to Marianne.

He repeated some of the things he'd written his daughter in his letters, though spoken here they sounded, he had to admit, like what one might read every day in the newspapers of the DDR.

The bucktoothed girl looked bored by it all, the husband indifferent, and the niece's face showed disdain. Lusk looked toward his daughter's large, sympathetic eyes to see if she believed he'd something valuable to say, but she seemed bewildered. He went on, and the words left his mouth and rose toward the Man in the Moon, without reaching any other ear.

Marianne Steiner's husband leaned over his wife, and toward Lusk, about to tell him that he was the usual petit-bourgeois excrement. He took a biscuit instead, but Lusk had lost his way, wandered back to the interrogation rooms and faces that despised him. "Rededication to Lenin . . ." he heard himself say. "And foreign enemies." He was running out of breath. "And even our slave labor," he said, "will become a benefit to the Socialist world now that the party has reformed itself."

Marianne Steiner looked disgusted with him, as if he had shat his britches. After all, she already had confessions that proved his words were lies. Lusk careened toward the wall he'd never reach. He dug his nails into his hands to stop the trembling. When he returned to the world, he'd blood on his right palm, and Marianne had disappeared.

"It's not easy for her," Marianne Steiner said.

He wiped his hands on his pants and went to look for his daughter.

Not a long search, as she was, as always, reluctant to leave the flat. She sat on the edge of the claw-footed bathtub, face contorted, as if engaged in some battle with itself. An incongruous pink shower curtain, decorated with shepherdesses and lambs, hung bunched to her side.

Lusk sat down next to her and pressed her close. The warmth helped keep him still, but he could see from her face that it had done nothing for his daughter.

"You're like one of West-West's villagers," she said, in half-swallowed words.

It was a phrase from the lexicon that Dora had taught them both. She meant that whatever the Castle might do, the villagers made it seem part of the inevitable order of things.

"Even if the party turns you into a slave, you justify it," she said, the words coming in a rush, "even if your legs are . . ." But at that she began to cry.

For him or for herself? He took a washcloth from a wire rack beneath the sink and began to dab lightly at his daughter's face.

She stopped crying, calmed by the touch of the moist cloth, or perhaps so she could better accuse him. "Your indestructible party is only bewildered and terrified men."

He recognized his words about Kafka from the hospital where his mother lay dying. His daughter wanted to tell him that *he* was the one who'd made fallible men into a god—and that meant he'd been a hypocrite about Kafka, which was, he knew, among the worst things a child might say about her father. Much he might say in argument to that, but more than being right, he wanted to reconcile with his daughter. "I can see," he said, "that I might have sounded like I'd made the party into a god."

"Not just *sound*."

He needed to find a more peaceful place for the two of them, and that depended, he knew, on his honesty. "No, you're right. Not just sound. I wanted the party to be more than human."

She studied Lusk's face. *This* father didn't know that honesty was above all. He lied to himself. This *man* could never protect her.

She was, in her way, a skilled interrogator. "When I was younger," he said, "I was insecure. I wanted there to be a power that could say I was substantial, something more than papier-mâché."

She blew her nose into the washcloth and handed it back to him. It felt oddly trusting. "I can see now," he said, by way of an offering, "that that must be why the man hit me in the eye with a pick." Though he saw the result every moment, it had been years since he'd remembered the blow.

"You can see it now," she said, "that you don't have the eye?"

That sounded almost friendly, made him feel he was on the right track with her. "It couldn't have been that he thought I was a snitch," he said, and he wondered why he hadn't thought of this before. "Why would he care about that? He was one, himself. No, it had to be because he'd heard me reverently say Lenin's name. He knew I thought my pious attitude made me different from him and the others." Even in the general destruction, he'd dreamt, he'd be the one who continued to believe, and because of the faith clung to within the whirlwind, he'd someday be reinstated by a purged, a renewed, Communist Party.

"And you have been," Marianne said. She still had a small hope that her father might somehow move from willing slave to master again.

To Lusk, though, she sounded like she wanted to comfort him, and that sense of a kindly presence made him feel that if he could only be more honest with her—with himself—he might build something lasting between them. "But when the party admitted its errors," he said, "it made things worse for me, made me feel hollow again."

His daughter looked toward him with bewildered eyes, and mucus all over her face. He wiped it from her cheeks, and threw the washcloth into the sink. "Your grandmother believed Khrushchev had given the people the truth. He'd revealed Stalin the schemer, told the world of Stalin the slave master, confessed to Stalin the murderer." Once, he'd needed to protect his mother, so she would not think she'd led her sons to slaughter; now that she was gone, he felt himself in the grip of an almost physical insistence to speak. "My mother was wrong, Marianne. Khrushchev had lied. He'd been complicit in the murders. They all had." Lusk, sadly, could hear that he sounded like the one who'd been crying, even if he'd run out of moisture some years ago. "And it wasn't Stalin who smashed my legs with a rubber pipe."

"The men who beat you obeyed his orders, though," Marianne said. She hoped her father couldn't tell she'd only been half-listening, lost in terror now that she knew her father's protection was worthless, that she'd soon feel the indecipherable electrical script tormenting the nerves in her legs.

"I understand fear," Lusk said. "I expect cowardice. It was something more than that. They wanted to hurt me." Lusk saw his torturers' hammerlike faces, each man as they beat him enjoying the peace of the corpse while still alive. "You were right, Marianne, the Communist Party is only bewildered and terrified men. And those men wanted to surrender their conscience; they longed to serve a brutal god."

"Why?" she said, because she could tell he'd wanted her to ask. Her only real question, though, now that her father had revealed his weakness, was what she might do, so her mother would forgive her betrayal and protect her again.

Lusk felt the answer to his daughter's question rise out of his body, as insistently as a baby's wailing. "Because no one," Lusk said, "lives even a moment outside terror for his life. We want a god who will order us to fire a bullet into another man's belly, so we can feel the master, even if only for the length of the victim's scream."

At which he felt his body relax, as if he'd finally let go of a dream of freedom and equality so long and rigidly grasped, and had found peace in thinking that the only earth ever to be was one populated by butchers and those about to be butchered; and the only equality was that they sometimes changed places.

That's a mood, he could hear his mother say, *not a world-view,* though perhaps out of consideration for Kolyma she wouldn't have said *mood.* Still, she was right. There must be a way out of the abattoir, Lusk thought wearily, only he was too old and damaged to find it.

Still, he didn't need to tell his daughter any of that. Instead, he gave her shoulders a squeeze.

That touch made Marianne's muscles rigid. Her father was a hollow man who'd easily been made into an accomplice and a slave; he couldn't help her, and their closeness could only drive her mother away.

Lusk stretched his legs and wondered how those who'd once rolled up their pants for him felt today, the few left alive. That their limbs had looked so much like his had been a thing he couldn't bear that day in the Lubyanka. Today, though, he'd wanted to repair his relationship to his daughter, and had ended up surrendering the party; he'd finally become one of them, one of the numerous.

Good for him. But it still left him feeling empty. Sad, too, because, *like any father,* he also wanted to be someone his daughter would remember proudly after he died. Or at least remembered for something *in particular* about his life.

"You're like the tattooed man," she said, getting up from her perch.

Meaning what? Was it a figure from some hateful story of Kafka's he hadn't read? "I don't understand."

"Your body, I mean. It has the history of the century written on it."

Thus his daughter resolved the contradiction for him: he was singular because his flesh had been maimed by so many mass experiences. More than most—a certain writer, say—where blood had flowed, his had flowed, too. There were several such, of course, as there were of everything; still, he supposed, it was something.

When they left the bathroom, they found the other guests had discreetly departed but hadn't cleaned up. The two of them washed and rinsed cups together. Marianne, lying, mechanically talked of maybe studying nursing again, when she really wondered how she would even manage to walk to the greengrocer. "The buses . . ."

"I remember. Jonah's whale," he said, with, he hoped, the proper touch of irony.

"You think I sound like *him*, don't you?" She was not, however, the least displeased by that. The more *he* saw himself in her, the more her mother might be drawn back to her.

Lusk felt exhausted by his confession, but he still managed to see something more he might gain from it, for his daughter's well-being. An exchange: *my god for yours.* "Kafka tells us to hate ourselves," he said, "and the party orders us to brutalize others. You and I have to give up those gods, Marianne; we have to find our own way now."

She wanted to slap him for that, so he'd remember that *first father* was no god for her, and never had been. And also to show where her loyalties lay—with her mother, and the man who wasn't a god to her, who her mother had loved. But no, her mother (at least when she'd lived with first father) hated violence. She gave Lusk a quick peck on the cheek, and a pat on the back when his cab arrived.

V

1

NATALIE LOOKED DOWN at Lusk from the top of her concrete stairwell.

"You're laboring badly," she said. "You need to see a doctor." She turned, though, before he reached her, and went back into her flat.

"The Stasi called me in while you were away. *Why England?* they asked. Who had you seen there beside your daughter? What bitter things had you said to them about the DDR?"

Lusk went to the couch to rest from the climb. "My advice is sign the first confession offered, if it's not for a capital crime. Otherwise, the ways they torture you to get your signature will kill you, as they have me."

That nonsense painted her thin face clown white. He told her of the mathematician from his first cell.

"It's good advice," she said. "It's what I did before."

He understood what she'd confessed about herself, and

how little he knew of her. But then, the last week had also shown how little he knew of himself. "As I did," he said.

"But your legs?" she said, without consideration.

"Perhaps not the first confession. But I sacrificed the same people in the end, a whole institute of them."

She embraced him, by way of comfort, he was sure, rather than congratulations. Still, she added, "We shouldn't see each other anymore. I couldn't—"

He understood; the Stasi had sent her careening toward her wall. The Law, he thought, is that each one must be alone among the shards and scrape their own skin only.

He made his way back to the stairs. Both the steps and the loss turned out to be more painful than he expected, and they both led downward to darkness.

2

IT MADE HIM FEEL he'd no time to waste, and when he got home, he set to work reminding Marianne of the imagined bargain, *my god for yours.*

No, Franz's hold on his Franziska was too strong for a mere exchange. The only thing that would work in his daughter's case was to have the god himself tell her that she must stop worshipping him. Lusk's hatred of Kafka had outlasted his love for Dora, but to save his daughter he would have to let that man's spirit invade him, take him over.

I remembered something you said when your grandmother lay dying, he wrote, *and it reminded me of a passage in a diary of Kafka's the Gestapo seized that has never been recovered:*

The indestructible is a fragile, and shy thing, always partly hidden. You have to devote your life to finding it. No doubt this is because if you thought you had found it, taken possession of it, you would command others in its name, and so pervert it.

And who knows? Perhaps it's our *search* that gives the indestructible life, and gives us life at the same time.

No, that last line was sentimental; Marianne wouldn't believe that it had come from Kafka. He crumpled the paper and took out a new sheet. He pushed on, though becoming this man, even to put an end to him, humiliated Lusk; it wasn't Trotsky, he thought, but Kafka who ended up fucking him in the ass.

I remember something from a diary of his that was seized by the Gestapo and never recovered:

An author's greatest fear should be that he might be mistaken for a wise man. And how much worse that would be if the author knows that all he has to offer is the knowledge that a man benefits most from a special sort of pilgrimage, a search that looks to the uninitiated like wandering. And to the initiated as well.

Each person's path is used up in the walking, if the person has the courage to take it; or its wasted, if he doesn't—for it was a path only for that one person. So no way can be known from the first, and none can be repeated.

Like all of Kafka's work, the specific injunctions seemed at once vague, and from a wintry medieval world. Would she understand that when *his* imaginary Franz wrote of pilgrimages it meant she should take buses to work, and lovers into her bed? For of all the many good things he once wanted for his daughter, what Lusk wanted now was only that she venture out of her flat a little more, and he wanted this, oddly enough, despite all the terrible things that leaving his room had brought to Ludwig (Lusk) Lask.

The worst disaster for such a writer would be if readers asked *the author* in what direction they should travel; after all, if someone knew the direction, there would be no point in your making the journey— it wouldn't be your path. And in any case, a writer would be the worst person to ask. Writing (is there such a thing?) shows nothing about an author's wisdom or character, except that he is the sort of person who can hold on to his desk at night in a strong sea, even with his teeth if necessary—and that requires only tenacity, and probably, also, a fear of water.

No, Marianne would suspect those lines, too. How could Lusk, she'd wonder, have memorized so much of Kafka? Or was he supposed to have copied it out and taken it with him to Kolyma, when everyone knew they hadn't been permitted even to keep their own underwear?

To make it believable that he could have remembered this, he had to make it shorter, reduce it to an aphorism. He methodically set to making a thick blackness over parts of each sentence. After that, he found himself filling in the curls of each *e* and *o* in the rest of it, before putting lines through all the remaining words. He blacked the spaces between the lines, obliterating everything, and made one solid rectangle that soaked through the page. At the bottom, he pointlessly wrote *Marianne, you* are *my heart,* and sentimentally didn't bother to throw the page away before he went to bed.

3

WHEN HE DIDN'T come to work for several days, Natalie Kolman, who still had a key to his flat, went to look for him. She knew it most probably hadn't been a broken heart that had kept him from the institute, but she found it easier to distract herself from her more major worry with a minor (if flattering) guilt.

She found him in his bed. Luckily, Lusk was neither her first lover nor her first corpse, and she could calmly look about the flat for anything left that might incriminate her.

Along the way, she found the black rectangle of ink, and the words about his daughter. A painting? Had he known to make a tombstone? Or maybe it was a way of taking the censor's pen from the Stasi's hand and using it on himself? There was an envelope next to it, addressed and stamped.

No work at all for her to send the letter. But what if the Stasi thought that enigmatic quadrangle was a code? Could they trace the letter all the way back to Natalie Kolman? On the other hand, mailing the letter gave her a way to make up for her cowardice—for the cowardice toward him, anyway.

Later, when Ludwig (Lusk) Lask was awarded the Fatherland Order of Merit for his service to the working class, and an honorary medal for forty years of membership in the party, she arranged that both those things, too, might be sent to Marianne Lask—not knowing that when Lusk's daughter opened this letter, it might undo all the good Lusk had hoped to achieve by surrendering his god for hers.

VI

1

MARIANNE NEVER OPENED ANY of the envelopes from Germany, just stuffed them far back in a drawer in her kitchen. It just wasn't worth the trouble to walk to a bridge where it would be safe to read them, as they probably contained only more of Lusk's pointless warnings not to make *first father* into a god, when *he*'d never been that to her, only a helpless man her mother had deeply loved. Marianne wanted to please *him*, yes, but only so her mother might come close to her again and protect her, as she had him, from the ghosts.

It was Marianne's misfortune to rummage for matches in that drawer nine years after the last letter had arrived and feel the edges of the envelopes she'd been so stupidly sentimental as to save. She slammed the drawer shut.

Too late. *We've always known you once turned to Lusk Lask for protection,* the more brutal one wrote. He always gave an extra charge to the nerves in her leg they used to form the script a painful education had finally taught her to read, though her profit on that was to compound the physical agony with shame for the things they wrote about her.

And to think that you would put Lask's letters—the second one added—*in the same place where you hid his picture when that pathetic slave, your real and only father, visited you.*

Was that particularly offensive to *him* or her mother, and actually, was that ghost a *second* one? She had thought so, because the pain this other one caused (if it was another one) was always so much worse. Maybe, though, it was just the same entity in different moods. She reminded herself that neither one of them (or the one of them) spoke for *him* or for her mother, or had ever offered her the least bit of useful advice.

Why would we? You're an excrescence on the earth, the first wrote. He'd become ever cruder and more insistent since she'd stopped taking the pills, berating her and poisoning her with black guilt but never saying what the guilt was for—to make sure, probably, that she couldn't make restitution.

You know what to do for that.

Not a long passage but a searing pain, because it meant: *You should die.*

She ran out the door without a coat, and toward the greengrocer—though she wondered why she should bother to run; after all, one couldn't escape from what had neither form nor place.

The people in the shop looked at her with faces as expressionless as hammers, or with contempt for a withered woman in her forties who, like an eight-year-old child, still needed her mother to smooth down her spiky hair, to remind her to wear a coat in December, and to protect her from demons. She was an object of all men's disdain.

Because you've never had a penis in your vagina, the first one explained.

She said aloud that she could reduce them both (or the one of them, if that's all there were) to an annoyance no worse than a rash just by taking the oblong pills the doctors had given her the last time she'd given up on her own methods. "This is all a simple mistake in biochemistry," the doctor had said. "Ghosts are only bad chemicals in the brain."

But you know better, the kinder one explained, as if to a child, though a child whose legs he wanted to hurt. *You know the material world always reaches to the other realm. Ghosts are chemicals in your brain, because the chemicals in your brain are ghosts.*

And the other brute wrote in letters of infinite hatred that if she took pills, she might not feel their messages in her legs anymore, but they'd cover her world in a veil again, and make her body tremble uncontrollably, just the way they had before.

Marianne managed to give the white-haired man in the smock the last of the month's benefit money in exchange for a week's worth of turnips, beets, and carrots. The grocer maybe remembered her from a time when her hair was well cut, her tweed skirt and blouse cleaner. He smiled at her and said, "These are all things that keep their heads in the ground."

Was that a pleasantry or an accusation? She looked at the pavement all the way home, so as not to see the Christmas decorations, rejoicing at the birth of a child that had been a gift to the world.

．　　．　　．

Her dinner was a plate of the uncooked roots, and she chewed each bite slowly, as *he* had, grinding each mouthful down till it lost all flavor before swallowed, a lonely, methodical, and slightly repellent enterprise even for her. How could her mother have loved that? But she had, so Marianne did it, too, praying it would bring her mother closer tonight.

Because after dinner, she must sleep, and almost every night since she'd stopped the medication, she'd wake at three, covered in sweat, sure that the terrible thing she'd done had been revealed in a dream that she could no longer remember.

The punishment for pretending not to know your crime will be added to that for your crime, the more brutal one wrote.

What difference would an additional punishment make, she said to him, when they'd already decided on a capital sentence for her?

The vicious one increased the voltage, shocking her with *shit-brain, stupid cunt, bastard,* and *bitch,* to demonstrate that the time between dying and dead could itself be made into an ever-worsening punishment.

The next night she saw how she might please him (and so please her mother) by doing the very thing that he'd most wanted done before he died. She put his picture by the edge of the sink, fanned the pages of her mother's copy of *Der Prozess,* and lit the edges. She dropped the book in the sink.

No luck. That charred only a few pages, but still some-one banged at the door, shouting that she was trying to destroy the house. This was wrong, but the voice also accused her of not having paid her rent for two months, which was true. He sentenced her to leave this place in one week.

In the loudest voice she could still manage she promised that she'd be gone by the end of the month.

How could she have said that? How would she find another place without her mother's help? In fact, without her aid, how would she even walk through the door again to get groceries?

A few nights later, she wrote the milkman a note to stop delivery (because *he* hated waste) and she made out a last will, not because she would need it—she certainly didn't mean to kill herself, and had nothing worth distributing, anyway—but she wanted her mother to see how very des-perate things had become.

That night, her tormentors woke her by making her limbs jerk up and down like a spastic puppet's. *You've made your will. It's time for excrement like you to vacate this flat and this planet.*

Don't worry, though, the less brutal one wrote. *I've made this journey myself. It's as easy as taking a long train trip.*

But Marianne wouldn't be gotten rid of so easily. She'd come up with a much better plan than filling a cup with hair or charring *his* books. *She'd become the character in his story who stopped eating and drinking altogether.* She wouldn't hold herself back from the common crucifixion. "That will make my kidneys fail," she said aloud, so her tormentors would think she'd taken the whip from their hands and had begun to punish herself.

It was all a ruse. She was sure she'd please *him* by starving herself to acknowledge she felt she couldn't ever please him—which was just the kind of convoluted thinking *he* savored most. He would smile on her, and her mother would come to her; she'd surprise her tormentors by leaping up again, brandishing her fist at them, having become Marianne once more.

After a few days without food and drink, the little left of Marianne felt desperate to go on living. She longed for a glass of water, but she didn't want to betray a plan that she was sure was just on the point of success.

You're being foolish, the kinder one wrote. *You can't please a man who hates himself by imitating him. He'll never adopt you as his child—*

—which you know, the brutal one wrote, *is the one your mother truly wants.*

Had she known? Of course, she must have. And as self-deception was what *he* and her mother both hated most, she felt as though she'd covered herself in her own urine.

Exhausted, she lay down on the floor and closed her eyes. She hoped for even a stuporous sleep, but the cold coming up her dress kept her awake. On the train, that chill would mean snow on the ground outside, and if she was lucky the snow would soon be so deep that they couldn't move forward anymore and would have to remain in their compartment.

The wind through the train windows continued to

sneak up her nightgown and made her teeth begin to chatter. Her mother tucked a shawl around her so she might sleep warmly through the night. She felt scratchy wool on her bare legs. She mouthed the word *blue* but said nothing out loud; she suspected the snow, the train, the blanket, the feeling was a fever dream and that she mustn't speak or open her eyes, or even the last blue possibility might disappear forever.

2

AFTER MARIANNE'S CORPSE had been lowered into the ground next to her mother's, the two mourners—Kafka's niece and the old Yiddish writer, who had, just as he feared, buried almost everyone he knew—strolled for a few minutes in the nearly empty cemetery. The ground was hard underfoot, and the air cold enough to show itself before their faces.

"Poor Marianne," Kafka's niece said. "She was probably more representative than she knew. Trapped between the worship of a spirit who offers garbled guidance, and a materialism sure it knows the way forward."

"And then leads one to the wall," Isaac said. "You know, I met her father before the war. But I'm re-formed by age now, and he didn't recognize me." He smiled. "I'm all ears," he said, and pushed one outward. "Her father lectured on Marxism to my agitprop group, and I had dinner once or twice at his family's very nice house. The girl's father, by the way, was ferociously jealous of your uncle."

"As was my father," Marianne Steiner said. "He felt he couldn't compete with his brother-in-law."

"There's a lesson in that. If you ever meet someone who has known an angel, you should run away from her as fast as you can." With difficulty, he took two long, high steps, but his old legs had begun to hurt again where they'd been broken long ago, and he returned to a methodical shuffle.

"Dora did have that air to her," Marianne Stein said. "More even than my mother. I mean, that she felt she'd encountered a supernatural being."

"Like Mary," Isaac said. "Except that the ghost forgot to make her pregnant."

"It felt like Dora had decided to spend her life reflecting on what she'd received. My mother had something of that about her, too."

Isaac stopped to peer at the inscription on a grave, whose numbers summed to a short life. "Probably Dora shouldn't have married again."

"Or had a child," Marianne Steiner said, with compassion, though for herself, mostly.

"She seemed very dedicated to this girl, though."

"Yes, but even an infant," Marianne Steiner said, quoting her own analyst, "requires that her mother need her a little bit, too, or she'll be crushed by her own wanting."

"That dinner in Berlin," Isaac said, "the one where I met Marianne's father, Brecht was there, also. The Lasks might not have known any angels, but they were an important family." He stopped by a stone to get his breath.

"Maybe better if Dora had married Brecht," Marianne said. "I'm told no one ever thought he was a saint."

"Oh, the Great Seducer would have fucked her, but he wouldn't have married her. He liked her breasts, I remember, but he feared her acting. Too hand on heart, O Schmerz! Schmerz! Schmerz!"

"One can understand his fear." Marianne Steiner smiled at Isaac's warbling cry. "After all, once one starts to wail, when will it ever end?"

"Should it end?" Isaac said. "Isn't it a fine thing for man to say just that to his dear friends." And once or twice as they walked along in silence, the old man bowed to the occupants of the graves and fondly, if mockingly, mouthed the words again.

MILENA JASENSKA AND
THE WORLD THE CAMPS MADE

1

ON OCTOBER 19, 1941, the Senior of Reception Block 7 brought Eva Muntzberg, the Senior for the Jehovah's Witnesses, a note from a political prisoner, Inge Heschel, who that week had been transferred with a hundred others to Ravensbrück Concentration Camp.

Eva Muntzberg had met Inge Heschel a year before, in the holding cell in the Alexanderplatz Gestapo Prison, where they'd been held with other politicals, Jews, race defilers, lesbians, and other asocials, mostly prostitutes, all of whom babbled anxiously of their coming transfers—though it had seemed to Eva that their chief worry hadn't been beatings, hard labor, or the likelihood of starvation but that anyone found with lice in her hair would have her head shaved down to the skin. Many of the women had shrieked at the prospect.

Eva Muntzberg had already spent three years in Stalin's labor camp in Karaganda—including three months in solitary—and her interest had narrowed to those things necessary to her survival. Hair had been useful once; on the steppes, a man had liked her and had shown her the proper way to weed so she wouldn't break her back; but she didn't believe it would help her anymore; the Gestapo would be as brutal but more rigorous than the Soviets, and all the other inmates would be women. Besides, desire was farther from her now than memories of infancy.

Still, those in the cell paired off and searched each other's scalps for nits, and though Karaganda might have diminished Eva's interest in her (or anyone's) appearance, it had also taught her never to stand out. She'd partnered with Inge Heschel, whose name Eva had recognized as that of a famous political philosopher who'd studied with Husserl and Heidegger but who had become a Marxist, and even for a time a party member.

Eva had spread the strands of the professor's graying hair, and in response to Inge's questions, had told her about her experience in the NKVD prison in Moscow, in the labor camp, and of Stalin's latest betrayal.

Inge's questions made Eva think that she might be one of those who'd already had suspicions of Stalin, yet couldn't believe they'd been lied to by the party whose structure Lenin had made flawless, and whose goal was humanity's only chance to survive. Such people remained always unsure about the truth, like a quivering compass needle. Eva's account today wasn't much more than a bare recital of events, but the needle had finally pointed north, and Inge began to weep. "We've sacrificed ourselves," Inge said, "and for what? What is there to live for now?"

Eva didn't know how to respond. In 1928, in Berlin, a court had given Eva's first husband and his family custody of her child; the court said her commitment to the party and to her lover, the party leader Paul Muntzberg, made her a negligent mother. In 1938, Stalin's courts had taken both Paul and the party from her, and she'd been sentenced to hard labor in Karaganda. In an isolation cell there, and without her willing it, Eva had become hardly more than a small spot of consciousness, a thing of minimal want (so as not to be fooled by hallucinated bread), and minimal caring for those outside herself—to better bear the loneliness; and so, more or less, she'd remained. "We live," she said to Professor Heschel, "in order to go on living," a tautology that, not surprisingly, didn't stop Inge's weeping.

Eva, though, had nothing to add, or perhaps not sufficient interest in adding it, and Inge went on with her crying while Eva went on combing through her hair and crushing the lice between her ragged nails.

In Ravensbruck, Eva had the green insignia of a Block Senior, which made it possible—though with some risk— to visit the new arrivals during their exercise hour, and, since Inge might be an ally here, a place where she had very few, she made that effort.

She spotted the small philosopher at the back wall of the camp, and she was glad to see that Inge hadn't had her hair cut off; she wouldn't have any additional reason—beyond Eva's having destroyed her faith in Stalin—to resent Eva. Another woman, taller and younger, who dragged one foot when she walked, made her way alongside Inge, and both stopped when Eva approached. "Milena from Prague," the tall woman said, and extended her hand. "Please don't give me one of your German handshakes. My joints are terribly swollen."

Eva took the woman's palm. It felt pleasantly warm, but Eva had seen two women who'd held hands beaten to the ground in front of this wall, and the shorter one of them had died of the wounds to her spleen. She dropped Milena's hand. Still, Eva's spirit rose to the surface for a moment, and even looked about. The tall woman had a prisoner's pallor already—the Gestapo's jails, no doubt—and her boots were too large for her.

Even that much looking made Eva feel nauseated, like a starving man who ate too large a meal. But before her spirit retreated, she said, "You look like a scarecrow." Eva was surprised by her own words, and that there had been words at all, but Milena laughed at them in a companionable way.

The path where they stood was a thin strip between the back of the barracks and the high masonry wall topped with electrified barbed wire. The inmates had to walk in a dreary line for the full exercise period, breathing the dust made by their own boots as they walked in a dreary line for the full exercise period. Even the guinea pigs who had been given gangrene in experiments at the infirmary had to lug themselves about on their crutches.

Women tried to push by them, one or two of them kicking at Eva's calf—these were probably the party militants among the newcomers, already briefed by the comrades about Eva's "lies." Milena ignored the other prisoners, and her attitude struck Eva as entitled and presumptuous, but also fascinating, as if Milena thought she was still a free creature.

After a few moments, the three walked together with the others, and Eva was conscious of Milena's right hand by the side of her dress. It made a slight perturbation in

Eva's spirit—a reminder of similar foolishness in the past. She'd grown fond of the man in Karaganda who'd shown her how to chop weeds, and his death had made her forget the simplest things. Someone had stolen her boots, and her feet had gotten sores that had become infected.

The Czech woman had been a famous left-wing journalist, and though Inge had told her Eva's story, she said she wanted to hear directly from her that Stalin could really have betrayed every internationalist principal and delivered antifascist refugees over to Hitler. "I like to ask questions myself," Milena said, "an old habit—"

"That liked you," Inge said, "and stayed and never gave notice," Rilke being to Inge, Eva supposed, what hair had been to the women in Alexanderplatz Prison, the thing that she must not lose if she were to remain herself. To Eva, Rilke's poetry was another thing, like hair, for which she no longer had a use.

As to Milena's questions, Eva knew she'd gain nothing from answering them. When she'd first arrived at Ravensbruck, she'd talked honestly about the slave labor camps, and the Communists took their revenge in ways as dangerous as spreading lies about her (to the inmates they said she was an informer, to the SS that she was a dangerous malcontent) and as petty as kicking her calves when History offered them the chance. But she saw a testing look on Milena's face, and though she didn't know what capacity Milena felt she was examining, or by what right, she responded, "Yes, that is what the party of the Workers' Fatherland did to those who took refuge there from fascism."

Milena asked more questions, and Eva had gotten as far as her flight to Moscow with her husband, a candidate for the Central Committee of the Internationale who'd dis-agreed with Stalin, though that may not have mattered very much in his arrest. Everyone substantial had been swept up, and, as in her case, many who weren't.

But before the NKVD came for her, the siren sounded at Ravensbruck, the guards began to shout, and the dogs yearned forward on their chains. Milena turned as she rushed away, and said that she hoped Eva would come again to tell her more of her story.

She doubted it. Even with the green armband, she would need a plausible excuse if a guard stopped her, and if the guard didn't like her story, or her manner, or was in a foul mood, she could lose her position as Block Elder, and even be sent to an isolation cell in the Punishment Bunker, where she knew she would retreat the rest of the way inside herself, and even the last, small remnant of Eva would disappear forever.

Still, the possibility that this woman wanted to hear more had reminded her of a time when she'd still occasion-ally felt the absence of a friend, a time before she'd learned that any organism may at some point need your ration of food more than your companionship. And that night, as the Witnesses slept or prayed quietly, she heard herself say *Milena* aloud.

2

FIVE MORE TIMES THAT WEEK, Eva took the risk needed to walk with Milena underneath the wall with the death heads painted on it. They were almost always joined by Inge, though the older woman said little.

Milena never mentioned her own hands again, or the hunger that all newcomers felt (which was, by the way, much less than it had been at Karaganda), the pain in the legs from work, and from standing in rows for hours morning and night to be counted and recounted, or the savagery of the guards if you strayed from your row— all the things about which new prisoners complained until they saw that the same pain already filled every other consciousness to the brimming point. Instead, Milena asked Eva more about her arrest, the prison in Moscow, the camp at Karaganda, and Eva answered, though to her own ears her account was like the rest of her existence: distant, colorless, and at once frightening and boring.

It was to Inge's taste, though. One could tell, she said, that Eva had seen the emptiness of all the goals of this world. "Eva's like Franz Kafka," Inge said. "Or his Hunger Artist."

"Who's Franz Kafka?" Eva asked, though she did not much care.

"Franz Kafka," Inge said, "was a great writer."

"And he was my lover," Milena said.

Apparently, that was momentous; Inge stopped walking and was pushed into Milena by some other prisoners, but she had the good sense to jump away, as if Milena's body had been electrified.

Kafka, as it turned out, had been a Jew from Prague who'd written in German, and Milena had been his first translator into Czech. At the time, Milena lived with her husband in Vienna, and at first she and Kafka had corresponded about difficulties in his text; but her own pain had spilled over onto the page, and she began to write of her unfaithful, feckless husband, Ernst Polack, and Kafka had written of his loneliness and fear. In this way, they'd fallen in love. "He was not like anybody I'd ever known," Milena said. "He never took refuge in blindness, in enthusiasm, in some conviction, the way the rest of us do. He let everything hurt him directly. It was like Franz was naked while everyone else had clothes on."

Milena and this peculiar-sounding man had only ever spent a few days together in the flesh, and to Eva it sounded as if all they'd been able to do was embrace. The siren sounded before Milena could tell them the thing Eva was surprised to find that she was a little curious to hear—namely, why the two of them couldn't fuck.

3

FOR THE FIRST TIME, hearing Eva's story of Stalin's camps produced a good result for her listeners. Inge and Milena had become the center of a tug-of-war between her and the party, and the Communists had seen to it that Inge was made secretary to the camp supervisor, and that Milena got a place as a clerk in the infirmary. These examples of the party's benevolence were meant to prove that Eva must have lied about the nature of Communism, and so of Stalin; QED: the camps didn't exist.

To show the party that they no longer believed the Trotskyite's lies, the two of them were told to break with Eva completely, and though Inge didn't kick her when she passed by, she did dutifully turn away and pretend not to know her. Milena, though, continued to walk with her, which moved Eva deeply. No one had ever made a choice like that for her before; nor had she, in the past, chosen anyone, even her own child, over the party.

Milena said she did it because she needed to amass material for the book she'd decided she and Eva would write after the war, *The World That Was the Camps*. But that reason was nonsense. Milena couldn't write down any of what Eva said, and couldn't possibly remember it. The idea of a book must be meant to help Eva believe that the Nazis would be defeated, that the two of them would be still alive when the camp was liberated, and that the Soviets would not be the army to do that, in which case Eva would be arrested again, and probably shot. All of that was far more hope than Eva could manage.

Like most things that asked for a response from her, Eva felt Milena's questions as an annoyance, but each time Milena asked, she found that, to her surprise, she answered. Today she spoke of the transport that had taken her to Karaganda.

Milena stared up at the electrified barbed wire, where a gypsy had recently lost part of her hand as she tried to escape. "There are," Milena said, "no scarecrows in your stories."

It took Eva a moment to remember. "You mean no people like you?"

"No, not that." Milena shut her eyelids and stumbled forward. "What color are my irises?"

Eva didn't need to reflect. "Blue," she said.

Milena opened her eyes and smiled. "So at least we know that you can see."

Of course she could. But why would she want to?

"I'm going to come to your barracks tonight, after everyone's asleep," Milena said. She'd spoken of a visit once before, though Eva thought it only another hyperbolic way to assert her independence. "To the duty officer's room."

She meant the room kept free in case a Gestapo officer visited, though in Eva's barracks he rarely did; the Jehovah's Witnesses—prisoners of conscience, who could leave the camp simply by renouncing their ridiculous faith—gave no trouble, did their work with tick-tock regularity, and needed few inspections.

Eva knew women sometimes met in secret, and even that more women touched than were lashed for touching, but to do what Milena described sounded like a form of suicide—and of murder. Guards with wolfhounds walked the camp at night. When Milena was caught, the dogs would tear at her legs until she told who she was about to meet, and no love for another person or love for an image of one's self was as strong as the bite of a dog.

Milena understood the silence. "Don't you trust me?"

Eva had been tortured by the NKVD and the Gestapo, and could have replied, *I trust you as much as anyone, myself included,* but the siren sounded, and Milena made a point of rushing off before she could speak.

4

THAT NIGHT MILENA STOOD in front of Eva in the empty room and said, again, "What color are my eyes?" This time, she didn't close them.

"Blue," Eva said. "And they look as if Milena has a fever."

Milena waved the very idea away. "Tell me about *your* eyes."

"Eva's eyes aren't as bright as Milena's."

"But they're beautiful in their distant sorrow. What about your hands?"

"Eva's fingers aren't as long as Milena's." To see even this much felt like touching frostbitten skin.

"What color is your hair, Eva?"

"Eva's hair is drab black, while Milena's is glorious red."

There was almost no light in the room, but the word made Milena's hair *appear*—a fascinating and vivid color, or perhaps it was just that color itself was fascinating.

"Eva is foolish," Milena said fondly. "I love her thick, mysterious, jet-black hair."

Eva was glad it hadn't been cut off, and dismayed that she was glad.

"And what of Eva's breasts?" Milena asked.

Eva smiled, as hers were, indeed, more ample, though she'd lost so much weight that they sagged now. "Eva's dress fits better," she admitted. And it did; both because of what was left of her figure and because the privileges of the Block Elder included a nicer dress, and better quality linen for the apron. Good wooden clogs, too.

"And your breasts?" Milena asked again, but this time she gently stroked the sides of Eva's breasts through the cloth of the better-fitting dress. Desire returned with Milena's touch—here in the most improbable place. It must be, Eva thought, because they were a little less starved than they were in Karaganda.

5

DURING THE NEXT EXERCISE PERIOD, Eva brought Milena a small piece of bread "to stave off fever," but Milena waved it away. "I want," she said, "always to be the one who cares for you."

Perhaps true. And maybe in the infirmary it was easy for her to steal the food nurses must sometimes leave on their plates. In any case, Milena would only allow Eva to give her one thing, details from her past, though now when the telling became toneless Milena's questions became much more pointed—what did the cabbage soup taste like to Eva (a rancid water), what did you do when you menstruated (used strips of foul cloth), what was the size of the turnip you said you found and how many fed from it? These queries still felt like a fingernail jabbing into tender skin, but as the spectral fingernail was in some sense Milena's, it also felt erotic, bound up with, even an extension of, what had been their brief, halting, all-too-partial explorations of each other's bodies.

Today Eva described the winter in Berlin, when Paul and she had first met, and a street salesman's dirty black fingerless gloves. "He had a folding table with children's pajamas for sale spread out on it."

"What color were the pajamas?"

"Yellow," Eva said, and saw them in front of her. There'd been a hawk wind that evening, and she'd had only a thin brown cloth coat. "Very clean pajamas, too, as if unused. Paul thought the man must have stolen them from a truck, or how had he gotten a pile of children's clothes of such spotless yellow felt?"

Milena, as she sometimes would, repeated the last few words, and Eva followed on after, saying, "for my daughter," and she added, "by another man." The words made her almost fall to her knees. "She lives with him now, in Palestine."

Milena stopped, turned back, and opened her arms for Eva. The guard shouted, and they each moved away from the other. "You must meet me here later," Milena said. "After everyone is asleep."

That false hope angered Eva. "Don't be stupid. That would be suicide."

"Then imagine it now, while we walk, imagine that we're together here, and there's only enough light for us to see the outline of each other's bodies. I hold you, and stroke your hair, and say to you what you already know, that when you gave up your daughter, you also saved her life. She's in Palestine, where she's safe."

That might be, but Eva knew she would never leave Ravensbruck, and that her daughter would never know anything else of her but the caricature that her former husband and his family provided of a reckless, fanatical woman, who, at best, ignored her child, at worst endangered her.

Milena described her hand stroking Eva's hair, and made ridiculous predictions about Eva seeing her child again. By the time the siren sounded, Eva cried not for the loss of her daughter, but that, except in imagination, she would probably never feel Milena's touch again.

6

NO, SHE WOULD HAVE only the forced march next to the high wall, the choking dust, Milena's questions, and the details from her own life, each one coming into consciousness as if for the first time, bringing others in its train. The more colors and shapes Eva provided, the more of Eva's past and its pain returned to her, and the more, too, that the present showed itself, the squat barracks, the thick black truncheons, the hideous tension in the muscles of the guinea pigs' faces as the guards with those thick black truncheons forced them to swing themselves forward on their crutches in the choking dust. And the more the pain from what she remembered and saw, the more she needed to be with Milena, to talk to her again, to find details that would interest her, because only that allowed her to bear what she felt from the past or the present.

Was there any way to escape what she saw around her? Maybe she would tell Milena about a vacation her family had spent in a hut in Finland when she was a child. Once she began to speak she would remember all its details, and she might be able to escape there for a moment, to an inner room made from memory where she could rest from the pain of other memory and of Ravensbruck.

7

BY MARCH OF 1942, Inge Heschel felt confident in her usefulness to the Camp Administrator and often fell in step with them again. She was accepted without a word, because Inge was an interesting and clever old woman, and because one couldn't afford the pleasure of a grudge in Ravensbruck.

Inge's eyes had small pieces of cloudy membrane embedded in them, and Eva and Milena had to reach out sometimes to guide her away from obstacles. Her hair had gone from gray to white, and her expression was like Eva's when they'd first met. She usually said almost nothing, only listened to Milena's questions, and Eva's details, which today included a chipped knife with a grip of hard black rubber (that the man who taught her to weed had owned), noodles cooked over a fire of sheep dung (when her crew had to work nights on the freezing steppes), the growths on her sores that looked like little black mushrooms (when she had been a fool for love and lost her boots), and the huge turnip that looked like a hemorrhoid (and had miraculously fed her whole work team). Sometimes Milena would clap her hands at a detail, as if congratulating both of them. "I suspected that someone who'd hidden from the world the way you had," she said, "must have done that because she had a great sensitivity to it. You're like Franz in that way, though his hiding took a different form."

But with each object, Inge shook her head with disappointment. "It's as if," Inge said, "you're saying in the horror there was also *this*." She stumbled over a rut in the ground. "You're like Rilke now," Inge said. "You tell your details like something seen intensely stands apart from the destruction, as if they're the Angels of the Existent." She made a dismissive gesture, taking in Ravensbruck, but also the past, the future, air and light, and, apparently, Rilke, too, who she'd also once loved. "But, Milena, you at least should remember your Kafka. Nothing stands apart from destruction—not even the person who says that nothing stands apart."

Eva thought Inge was wrong. The details were indifferent, mute, and sometimes part of the horror; yet they were *present*. Just noticing them made her feel connected to that, even if she couldn't quite say what *that* was. Maybe it was endurance; when the things were destroyed—as they would be—something would *exist* still, however scattered and transformed. But when her consciousness ended, nothing would be left for her, so why was being's endurance a comfort to her?

Improbably, Inge smiled. She looked from Eva to Milena, trying to see—or to remember—their faces. "Or maybe," she said, "I envy the two of you and your game." She meant their love, and Eva worried it might be dangerous that that love was so obvious, even to the blind.

They talked of other things. Milena warned them not to go to the infirmary, even with a fever. She suspected that when everyone was asleep, there was a doctor and a nurse who went through the wards and gave some patients lethal injections.

"If it's the ones who had been bourgeois," Inge said, "then they probably do it to steal the gold in their teeth." She turned to Milena and spoke quietly but sharply. "Tell no one else. If you report them, you accuse the Gestapo itself. They'll shoot you immediately."

8

BUT WITHIN A WEEK, Milena had told the camp commandant, and perhaps because of a self-possession undimmed by Ravensbruck—though more likely for some reason of Gestapo politics they'd never know—she'd survived. The nurse and the doctor had been arrested and charged with stealing gold from the Reich.

And maybe because one can't live entirely in refusal and absence, at the beginning of June, Inge had altered a work list so that the guinea pigs would be spared jobs clearly meant to kill them. Inge's crime had been discovered almost immediately; the guinea pigs had been reassigned to suffer and die, the supervisor sent to prison, and Inge executed.

This reminder of how easily they both might die made Eva desperate to see Milena alone again, and she proposed that they use the confusion of the Sunday promenade, and meet in the infirmary, where Milena had said she could get a key to one of the consulting rooms.

Milena smiled. "Wouldn't that be suicidal?"

Did she want Eva to act like a lovesick teenager and say she didn't care? "I don't care," Eva said. And then added, as if she were sentencing herself, "Really, I don't care."

9

SUNDAY, JUNE 28, 1942, Strauss waltzes played through loudspeakers, and a thousand women walked in twos and threes through the central path wearing nearly identical striped dresses and white headdresses. Guards with police dogs strode back and forth through the crowd, seemingly in time to the music. A woman lay on the ground, trying to cover her head as a guard beat her and screamed at her for showing a strand of hair beneath her headscarf. Eva walked a little faster than the others, and a little to the side with each step.

Next to the latrines, two gypsy women swayed in each other's arms, while others stood guard and sang their own music. Eva remembered the once or twice she'd held women before Milena, but always so embarrassedly that she'd gotten no nourishment from it. Failed experiments, she'd thought; her life was only with men. And if today some thin skeptic were to say, *Ah, so Milena happened because there are no men here,* how could Eva reply, except with a tautology: her love for Milena was as great as her love for Paul had been, and stronger than any embarrassment, *because it was for Milena.*

But if Eva were to say that to Milena, she would wave it away as she had the bread. Instead, Eva would tell her about the acidic shit smell of the latrine that was like an ocean you could feel in your eyes and on your skin, and of the lithe twist of the starving bodies, so unlike the heavy gypsy dancing she'd seen in Berlin. That would lead naturally to telling of her grief for Inge, at which Milena would smooth her hair, until the stroking of her long fingers would almost make Eva forget Inge, Karaganda, Ravensbruck, and herself.

10

BUT MILENA LOOKED DISGUSTED and angry at her vignette of the dancers.

"They'd pushed the headscarves aside," Eva added, as if that might get her audience back. "It made them look like they were drunk."

That didn't help. Milena liked gypsies well enough, she said, but loathed their music, which had been playing day and night in the bar below her in the villa where she had tried to clean herself of a morphine addiction. It had begun after an operation for her leg injury. She'd drifted in and out of consciousness, and each time she had to come back to a world made nauseating by that awful Romany music.

"I couldn't have known," Eva said. Not about the music, or the ski injury, or the morphine, or so much else. She felt forlorn.

"Oh, God, I'm sorry," Milena said. "I'm not angry at you." She'd gotten a letter from her own daughter that day, and it had been, she said, a perfectly nice letter, a polite letter, but it had nothing in it but news of exams, and piano lessons, words written for the censors, when Milena wanted to know . . . she didn't know what—but something that would bring her daughter closer, let Milena feel her child's need, and her confusions. "Some details, something about boys, or about if she'd gotten her first stockings yet."

Milena wept. Eva took her into her arms and stroked her hair, glad that she was allowed to care for her this time, though she also, meanly enough, felt cheated.

Milena talked about her father, a doctor, who would raise her daughter now, "God save her. The man put me in a mental hospital to break up my relationship with a Jew."

"Kafka?"

"No, Polack, my first husband."

She couldn't help herself. "Why wouldn't he fuck you?"

The question made her stop crying, and Eva felt the joy of this accomplishment, felt it more sharply, too, than the times she'd helped her own child.

"Polack? From boredom. But really you mean Kafka. Everyone," she said, "means Kafka." Oddly, that made her smile. "He feared the flesh," she said, "but not like a neurotic—or, no, perhaps it's the way Franz said, a neurosis also has something true in it that the illness grows around, like a tumor."

In this case, that meant Kafka saw that we're animals with teeth; which was a funny thing to say, because of course many of hers and Eva's were already falling out.

"If people are going to fuck," Milena said, "they mustn't see each other's selfishness and violence so clearly. Franz, though, couldn't not see, and he couldn't lie to anyone, not even himself. So he still loved me, but he couldn't fuck me."

"Do you think *I'm* very blind," Eva asked, still stroking

Milena's hair, which had thinned a little and was streaked with gray.

"Do you mean do I think you don't see how vicious I really am?" She looked sorrowful. "Yes, Eva, you make too much of me, and maybe I of you. For example, I think you're as honest as Franz, even about yourself. But who knows, maybe I'm wrong about both of you." That made her smile. "But I can't really see how I could be wrong. I suppose it's like the eye not being able to see itself."

"It can," Eva said, "in a mirror."

"Well, that will be the book you'll write for me later. But I know now I won't be there to read it." Neither talking of herself or self-pity were like her, Eva thought; or perhaps she was lost in her illusions and didn't know what was like her anymore. The idea of Milena's absence terrified her.

The music outside was ending. She hurried to have more of Milena, and stroked her back, felt her ribs beneath her sweet, dry skin, and prayed that her touch might give Milena as much comfort as Milena's touch would have given her.

Her hands ran over Milena's ass and legs, and she felt the bones in Milena's thighs; that touch made both Milena's body and her own fingers present to her. She looked toward the opaque windowpane, and it undulated a little in her eyes like a lake rippled by wind. For a moment, she imagined that they were on a boat.

11

THEY WEREN'T. A few months later transports had come for the cripples, amputees, mental defectives, bedwetters, and asthmatics, and by the winter of 1942, they'd come for the gypsies and the Jews, a few of whom she'd heard try to deceive themselves about men's teeth, saying they might not be killed immediately, as they, unlike the cripples, were still capable of work. A day after each transport, the dead's crutches, socks, underwear, and Bibles had come back in the same trucks, present still, and painful to the eye. The SS piled them in the center of the camp, where the promenade had taken place, an outer room filled with details that had accompanied but had done nothing to save the cripples, the gypsies, the Jews.

At the beginning of 1943, soon after the last Jewish transports had left, thousands more Poles, Hungarians, and Czechs had arrived, but they hadn't been taken away to be gassed. Instead, they were stacked on large platforms at night, three levels of them to a bunker, and were worked to death by Siemens during the day, as rations were now as bad as they'd been at Karaganda. Still, the Slavs hadn't always died quickly enough for the Gestapo, and in the evening, when the Polish women lined up just across from the Witnesses, Eva had been close enough to see their lips move in prayer as the shots sounded from the alley behind the camp wall and crows rose from the roof of the commandant's house.

Had it been a compensation or comfort to her that she'd noticed the crows? Inge had surely been right that the details were not angels, answered no prayers, and wouldn't survive the general destruction; and yet she hadn't been able to take her eyes from the black birds until they settled back on the roof.

By May of 1944, the executions were almost continual, the corpses carted immediately to the new crematoria along with the hundreds of others who'd died each week from cold, and typhus, or starvation. The insignificant rations had been cut in half, the workday extended to eleven hours, and anyone who looked like they might not be able to labor hard—anyone too thin, or who had swollen legs or gray hair—was murdered and burnt. On her way to the infirmary today, she saw a few SS men lash some of the condemned forward across the space where there had once been a promenade, and the wraithlike prisoners' expressions and pace remained unchanged as they moved steadily to their end.

12

THEY PASSED. Eva climbed through the broken window at the back of the infirmary, into the latrine, and walked past the corpses stacked against the wall by the toilets. Any prisoner who came with a fever was told to rest in the hall till a bed was available, and during the night was given an injection of Evipan. The bodies mounted up and had to wait here for a week to be carted off to the fire.

In the corridor, Eva picked her way over those soon to be murdered, and went on to Milena's ward. Her friends already stood around her bed. Several of them had used a paste of water and soot to disguise their gray hair, in the hope they'd be able to avoid the ovens. Why would these frightened women care so much about Milena that they would risk being found away from their work, in order to make sure *she* wouldn't be given a lethal injection, even though her kidneys would certainly soon kill her. Had she stroked their breasts, too? Had she led them, too, back to a world that would become insupportable to them without her?

Milena gestured to Eva, who came forward and leaned toward her mouth, and Eva felt proud that the others were seeing her special place in Milena's heart. Milena told her to look after Jana when she died, tell her daughter that Milena had always kept her in her heart, and that she'd spoken of her every day in the camp.

Perhaps Milena thought that was true. Eva nodded yes, though it was foolish to think that she would live very much longer herself. Or would want to.

"And promise me you won't forget any of the details for our book."

"No," she said. "Of course I won't." Though once Milena was not there to make them supportable she would, she knew, pray that she might.

After that, Milena asked Eva to hold up some postcards her father sent with engravings of Prague scenes, so her homeland would be the last thing she saw. Milena stared at one and talked as if she and Eva were inside the picture, walking by the cathedral, the two of them and one other, a man who Eva thought must be Kafka. Milena said, "I want to pray." She sounded as if she were pleading for the chance.

"You should," Eva said. "I'll join you."

"No, I can't. You know he won't tolerate lies."

Milena cried—or so her eyes looked; she didn't have enough water for tears. Eva touched her withered cheek, but she could see Milena didn't see or feel her hand.

"He withholds himself," Milena said.

"Kafka, you mean? Or God?"

"Oh, both of them." Milena smiled with teeth that were almost completely brown, and died.

13

AT THE END OF 1944, about six months after Milena had died, a gas chamber had been built to destroy the Jews brought in from the death camps in the east that had been closed as the Soviets advanced toward Germany. The chamber's brickwork had a yellow tone that was like the felt that had done nothing to keep her child from being taken from her, the color now collaborating with the Nazis in murder, and Eva had understood why Inge had gestured at the whole skin of the world. Everything seen only added to Eva's nausea. She wanted to cry out, *Why did you call me to sight again, if this is what one sees?* But the person she wanted to cry to was dead.

For the next six months the Nazis fed the gas chamber night and day, and the smell of burning flesh pervaded the camp, growing stronger still as the Soviet Army approached Ravensbruck from the east. And then, in May of 1945, a year since Milena had died, most of the German prisoners were suddenly released, ordered to make their own way home.

14

EVA HAD GONE as fast as she could toward where she thought she'd find the American lines, and when she'd found them, she remembered that she'd stolen a bicycle, but not much more about the trip. With each kilometer from Ravensbruck, Eva had become more like what she'd been when she'd left the isolation cell in Karaganda, a woman moving in a world she could barely see. But she wasn't just as she'd been after the isolation cell, either, for she still had Ravensbruck inside, because she'd shared that place with Milena; and she had, too, the things she'd talked about that had come alive from her interest. Each memory was now the source of a harrowing pain. And when, against her own good sense, she would search inside herself for the image of Milena to help her bear that pain, her mind and body again discovered her death, and she would double over in grief.

And that was her existence for a year. Once or twice, thinking to feel even a flare of the present, she'd burnt her hand, or cut her arm with a knife, but that only scarred her body and stained her clothes. Eventually, someone gave her the name of a psychiatrist in Heidelberg who was not strictly Freudian—the Nazis had made sure no doctor left alive in Germany was strictly Freudian—but he was a sort of psychoanalyst nonetheless, and her friend claimed he'd had some success treating the severe depressions of those who had been interned in the camps.

15

THREE MONTHS into the sessions, her doctor said, "Perhaps your Milena thrived on people needing her as you did, depending on her in an almost desperate way, like a baby with its mother."

Eva saw Milena wave away the bread she'd offered her. *I want always to be the one who cares for you.* "And when she repeated the details of my life," she said, "was that like a mother feeding her baby?" She thought she'd been joking—or as close as she might come to that activity.

"Yes, precisely so." The doctor was a thin, fussy-looking man, who had a well-appointed neat office, which gave it an air of unreality, since there could be no such offices left in a shattered and occupied Germany. "Milena repeated the details, made them palatable to you by making them part of the maternal body, and then she nursed you with your own life. Each time, it bound you more tightly to her."

Her doctor believed that Eva's affection for Milena was why she still remained tied to a traumatic past (by which adjective he meant the way the German people, maybe including him, had conspired to murder whole nations, make her and thousands of others into slave-labor, and then had starved the slaves to death).

Like all love, he said, Eva's for Milena was love for a fantasy, an illusion; it was a vast overvaluation. Eva needed to analyze it, and break her destructive attachment to Milena and to the trauma of which she'd been a part.

And hadn't Milena, like the doctor, said that Eva made too much of her? She tried to see Milena clearly, as she supposed Kafka would have. She wanted to be healthy again, wanted one day to visit her daughter in Jerusalem, and not terrify the child by her soul's absence.

But for all efforts, what she saw, when she remembered Milena's gestures, wasn't moral flaws, but the beauty of the way she'd swept her long hand outward, the thinness of her arm, the generosity of her smile, the reality of her care. And what Milena had done with Eva's life seemed kind and intuitive, a method to take Eva's poisoned past and make it into food for her again. Despite all the doctor's mean-spirited interpretations, Eva's love for Milena felt undiminished, and the present as distant as ever.

"Our time is up for today."

Eva put on her coat.

"Have you written your daughter lately?" He meant, she thought, Please try to take an interest in a future, so you might have a present again.

16

WITHIN AN HOUR, she sat at a small wood table in a furnished room, over a café that served U.S. officers scalding but real coffee that the café owner bought on the black market, along with stale black-market pastries. She couldn't have told you if she'd taken off her coat yet, or what she'd thought or seen on her walk back to this room, except that, as always, the buildings, which had been left standing by the Allies during the War, had looked as insubstantial to her as the painted backdrop for a play; as if, in occupied Germany, only what was already destroyed could possibly have ever been real in the first place.

She looked down at the table and saw that she must have recently set a blank sheet of paper there, probably so she could, as the doctor wanted, reply to a child who had written page after page that was sympathetic to the situation of the unknown woman who called herself her mother, saddened by the horror she'd passed through, and horrified by the hatred she'd had to confront from those former comrades who had been her only friends. Her daughter didn't reproach her with once having sacrificed her to those same comrades, but instead said in each letter how much she wanted her mother to come to Jerusalem as soon as she felt well enough—though all of it, the sympathy and the invitation, always felt written to measure, probably under the direction of her former husband, or her unfailingly polite father-in-law, the same theologian who'd paid for the court case against her.

That memory made her feel like a weight had been dropped on her back, and she bent toward the table. Once Milena had said, *When you gave up your daughter, you also saved her life,* but this evening that only increased her grief, because Milena wasn't there anymore, and because in Jerusalem her daughter would know the truth: Eva hadn't given her child up to save her; it was the court that had rescued her child when it seized her from Eva.

That child was now a young woman of nineteen. She'd enclosed a recent picture of herself, and Eva lay the photo against a pile of her letters. Her daughter stood smiling beside her father, and the resemblance was striking—both of them tall, beautiful creatures, with longish faces and sorrowful Jewish eyes. If the doctor managed to return Eva to the present, would she see a resemblance to herself, as well? Was a mother who had abandoned her child allowed to see that?

For comfort, she picked up an envelope from a second pile, this one addressed in a careless, rushing hand, the pages inside smudged and ripped from being too often read. It was just the sort of letter the writer's mother had once said she wanted, pages desperate with need and confusion, and filled with details of the girl's life. And her letters always had some details, too, that could be added to

Eva's store of memories of Milena, as if Eva's life could now grow backward only, and, like some historian's book, only through the reports about the past from others.

She'd learned from Jana that Milena—the scarecrow—had once been overweight. Milena couldn't cook, and dinner was usually sausages on a plate. Milena wore a beret whenever she left the house but took it off as soon as any conversation began, and used it to gesture. Milena listened to the radio all night long, going from station to station, stopping even at those whose language she couldn't understand. Milena loved movies, and always took Jana with her, no matter how adult the subject. Milena would walk through Prague with her afterward, the two of them warming their hands from one chestnut seller to the next, and Milena answered all Jana's questions. Milena would make everything into a game, and when the electricity was cut off because they couldn't pay the bill, she put candles in bottles and went from room to room playing the Miller and the Child.

The details in Jana's letters were precious but didn't bring Eva closer to the present and didn't reduce the pain of the past, but only added to it, reminding her both how much of Milena's life she'd been excluded from and that that life was over. Yet more pain was at least *more;* and listing what she'd learned about Milena this evening was bitter, but also tonic; it gave Eva the strength and the resolve to try to fulfill the doctor's prescription to write her own daughter.

In the morning, though, she woke by the table, still in her coat, and the page still blank.

17

FOR WEEKS THAT SUMMER, almost every day brought alkaline yet sustaining words from Jana, who had begun to trust Eva more, and to speak more frankly about her life, and about her mother. The weight Jana had mentioned had come from Milena's morphine addiction; Milena's nervous fiddling with the radio was the anxiety of an addict who didn't have her drugs; the games in the dark had been fun, but the reason they couldn't pay the bill was because the money had gone to buy the precious cough tablets, which were kept in a tea set's yellow milk jug that sat on a sideboard.

Mother didn't suffer helplessly, though. She tried over and over to end the habit, and once had Evzen lock her in her room and keep the key. Within a few days, though, she waited till Evzen was out and shouted to me to get her more pills from the pharmacist, to do it within an hour, and to push them through the crack under the door, or she would jump out the window to her death. Can you imagine my fear in the taxi on the way to the pharmacy?

And, indeed, though Eva couldn't have told you the color of her doctor's hair, the yellow of that milk jug had a hallucinatory intensity for her, and though Eva could barely imagine the insides of the people near her, she could feel just as Jana had in the taxi, the anxiety vivid to her because it had been caused by love for Milena. And though she knew that what Milena had done was savage, it still didn't diminish her love for her, any more than it had that of the girl who wrote her about it.

After, she opened the other envelope, one addressed in a hand she didn't recognize.

18

"YESTERDAY," she told the doctor, "I got an anonymous directive that very much agreed with you. It said I shouldn't dwell on the past."

"Yes? I'm glad to hear that. But why anonymous?"

"Lack of courage. It warned me not to write a book about the supposed Soviet camps, because if I slandered the party, it would have to broadcast the truth about my collaboration in Ravensbruck with the Gestapo." She cared not much more about that lie than about anything else, but she wondered how they'd heard she might write such a book. "It had to be from someone in Ravensbruck with me." She paused. "Or maybe it was you, doctor."

The doctor laughed. "First of all, the threat is, I hope, a pointless one, because you could never be so depressive as to write a book that would only imprison you further in your own past. And when you level that ridiculous accusation against me," he said, "you indicate why you bring this up in the first place. You're looking for an excuse to run away from therapy."

The doctor didn't understand that it might be unhealthy for her to write the book, but that if the party found they could control her in this matter, there was no end to what they might demand from her.

Still, she dropped the matter and told the doctor instead about Jana's letters, most recently about how Milena had used her in party work, sending her to collect their illegal newspaper, despite the risk to Jana.

"I regret your writing *her* daughter," he said, "for the same reason I wouldn't want you to write that book. But perhaps there's something to be learned here. Milena never seemed to think about the consequences of her actions for Jana, or for you. Probably there was always something more important to her, her journalism, her Communist Party, her underground work, her drugs. But really, wasn't the real cause that everyone was meant to make sacrifices for Milena herself, and her own lust for experience?"

Eva felt a sharp pain in her stomach; a wayward desire to please this fussy man had made her betray her beloved. Still, what he had just said might well be true.

"I remember we talked of Milena as like your mother. Jana's letters might make you wonder if she was a good one for her own child, or for you."

And yet what Eva thought was that she, herself, would have been just such a mother to her own daughter, if the court had given her the chance. She'd have told herself that there was no sacrifice that one mustn't make for the worker's cause and the defeat of fascism, and used her to carry messages, perhaps, or to pick up papers. And when she'd fled Germany, she'd have taken her daughter with her to the Soviet Union, where, when Eva had been arrested, her daughter would have disappeared into a Soviet orphanage and died. Her husband's court case had saved her daughter from the Nazis, and from the child's own heedless, fanatical, and deadly mother.

This identity meant that for the first time since she'd begun talking to this doctor, Eva felt a disappointment in Milena that was as strong as her disappointment in herself, but when she looked about the doctor's office, it was no more present to her than before.

"For today," the doctor said, "our time is up."

19

THE NEXT WEEK, Eva began to talk about Jana's own dabbling with morphine herself.

The doctor interrupted her and asked angrily why she'd written to Jana again after he'd specifically ordered her *not* to do that.

She would have sworn that he sounded frightened.

"You never ordered me not to write her."

He called her a liar and said he couldn't go on treating her, that no one could, because she didn't really want to be cured of her attachment to Milena.

She sat up from the couch and turned toward him, and it was *his* ashen face that looked as though it had been slapped. As in a fairy tale, he'd shrunk in size, too. "The comrades," she said. "They've gotten to you, haven't they?"

For a moment, this good German must have remembered a bit of his better self. "You have to understand, Eva. You were in Ravensbruck—" As if to say, *That was your good fortune.* "There are certain things I had to do to survive out here that I wouldn't want anyone to know about, things my reputation—"

She left his office immediately, and felt almost giddy as she did, as if she'd been saved from a trap. This was the present her doctor offered her—men who were partial, boastful, craven, confused, and conquered, not one of them the equal of her Milena, who *hadn't* done the very thing her doctor had, betrayed her because of threats from Communists, threats not to her reputation but to her life.

20

AND HER DOCTOR'S COWARDICE meant she could rush to Prague, where she could counsel Jana, perhaps get her out before the Communists took complete control of the government. She bought the tickets the same afternoon. She walked home and imagined herself outside the cathedral in the postcard, where she would talk sternly but fondly to Jana. Later, she would confiscate the pills in the yellow jug and help get her ready to return to school with her in Germany.

But the day after she'd secured a visa, the party had taken over Czechoslovakia, and within a week, Jana sent a letter: *Please don't write me anymore.* Eva had wept for all the details of Milena's life she would never hear, but her tears taught her, too, that despite her imagined postcard lectures to Jana, Eva was herself not much changed; she had cared only about what Jana could give her.

Her own daughter had been fortunate that a court had taken her from Eva, and Milena's daughter was fortunate that the party had closed the door on Eva, who wouldn't ever be able to visit, and draw Jana back into the past, the two of them the last devotees of the cult of Milena. Best for Jana, for her daughter, for her former comrades, for her coward of a doctor, if Eva never spoke to any of them again. She didn't belong with them, or in the land of the living, but maybe only in a place carved inside herself, the hut in Finland, perhaps, where, even if you were capable of sight, there were nothing but fields of snow that asked next to nothing from you, and offered less in return.

Maybe she would settle in this hut and write the book she'd promised Milena, the one about the camps and about Milena. That could be Eva's world within the hut.

For God's sake, no, her doctor said, more agitated and concerned than she might have expected, though she supposed that in his imaginary form he didn't risk much by talking to her. *You mustn't lock yourself away with her. No one's worth that sacrifice.*

Well, at that, Franz Kafka, she imagined, would have responded with a companionable but bitter laugh, like brandy made into sound. He'd tell the doctor that he might know about others and the love they evoked, but he'd never understood their living flame, the reckless, caring, courageous Milena Jasenska, a woman in whom even the Hunger Artist had found his food.

Her death, Kafka would agree, would leave a sane person with only one wish left, and writing her and Milena's book would let Eva satisfy that desire, let her climb into the grave with Milena and all the things she'd given Eva, her long fingers stroking the sides of Eva's breast, the look of the startled crows, the yellow of a child's pajamas, the helpless wounding angels that would provide mute company as she and they were ushered out of life altogether.

Or, more likely, writing and revising would make her memories *less* painful and less vivid, leave the yellow paler, the crows more worn and distant, and Eva would emerge from the hut with a manuscript and years left to live, a woman mild and purposeless—except for the times when the comrades would slander Milena, and what was left of Eva Muntzberg would give them a sharp galvanic kick.

Eva didn't look forward to either ending. But in any case, to write a book, a person has to eat and keep warm. She got her coat, left her hut in Finland, and went down the stairs to a café in Heidelberg, to provision herself with some overheated coffee and stale pastry before she set to work.

AUTHOR'S NOTE

If one has the good fortune (is it good fortune?) to encounter Franz Kafka—in his fiction, in his diaries, in a biography, or in accounts by friends—one meets a sickly, anguished, very considerate man, a vivid, unsettling presence who had many profound (though usually not bitter) discontents—with language, with his father (oh, maybe that one *could* get a little bitter), with God, with politics, with his body, and with a great deal else besides, all lived out imaginatively, humorously, and mercilessly to himself, and sometimes, alas, to others. Nonetheless, Kafka had many fond friends, some of whom loved him deeply.

Their affection may have helped Kafka to bear, but not to resolve, his discontents, that, and, of course, his necessary, seasick experience of writing them, a task he took on as if it was rescue, or might lead there, even though, of course, he knew that there wasn't any such thing. Still, he set out again and again; maybe, if he embodied himself in a language that absolutely would not do but would have to, if he lived all of himself (which he also found *by* writing) as a question, he could keep moving in fiction and in life, if not forward, then around, like K. trying to find the way to the Castle, unsettled and able to unsettle others, yet truly eager himself to settle down, supposing that there was honestly someone anymore who might give him that right (though that *honestly* seemed also to guarantee, *never*).

His honest, stupendously self-critical attempt to answer those questions is his living presence; it provides an illumination of the intricacy of impossible predicaments, and an example of a sad, heroic persistence in what seem like ridiculous and necessary tasks. (For example, those moments when you might feel God is absent or dead, but you still feel a biting, inescapable remorse for which you have no way to atone and so set off to find Him again, or finally bury Him.) When you share that sort of mood—and his work is his way to bring about those unfortunate feelings in you, his way to make companions for himself—Kafka becomes encouragement, and, more than that, he becomes company.

The stories in this book have been meant as a way to express my gratitude for that company.

Which means I would also very much like to thank those who, along with Kafka (and his magnificent companion, Max Brod, who saved that work for us from his final self-punishment), made possible my encounter with him, with his friends, his lovers, and the horrifying times in which they lived and died. These include, though it's hardly a full list, Kafka's biographers, among them, again, Max Brod, and also Ernst Pawel, Nicholas Murray, Ronald Hayman, Louis Begley, and Reiner Stach. I am also very grateful indeed for *Kafka's Last Love: The Mystery of Dora Diamant* by Kathi Diamant, and for the accounts by those who knew Kafka, or knew those who had known him, most especially *Kafka's Milena,* by her daughter, Jana Cerna, and *Milena* by Margarete Buber Neumann, memories of memories of those thankful for their intimate contact with this troubling, vivid, and seemingly impossible fellow.

In fact, even now, I begin to doubt such a person ever could have been, and must hurry to return to his stories, and the stories about him, to reassure myself that he existed, and exists.

A NOTE ABOUT THE AUTHOR

Jay Cantor is the author of three novels,
The Death of Che Guevara, Krazy Kat, and
Great Neck; a graphic novel, *Aaron and Ahmed:
A Love Story* (with James Romberger); and
two books of essays, *The Space Between*
and *On Giving Birth to One's Own Mother.*
A MacArthur Fellow, Cantor teaches at
Tufts University and lives in Cambridge,
Massachusetts, with his wife and daughter.

A NOTE ON THE TYPE

This book was set in Monotype Dante,
a typeface designed by Giovanni Mardersteig
(1892–1977). Its first use was in an edition of
Boccaccio's *Trattatello in laude di Dante* that
appeared in 1954. Although modeled on the
Aldine type used for Pietro Cardinal Bembo's
treatise *De Aetna* in 1495, Dante is a thoroughly
modern interpretation of the venerable face.

Typeset by Scribe
Philadelphia, Pennsylvania

Printed and bound by Berryville Graphics
Berryville, Virginia

Designed by Maggie Hinders